This is a work of fiction. Names, characters, businesses, places, events and incidents either are the product of the author's imagination or are used fictitiously. Any resemblance to actual persons, living or dead, events, or locales is entirely coincidental.

Copyright © 2020 by David J. Hamilton

All rights reserved. No part of this book may be reproduced or used in any manner without written permission of the copyright owner except for the use of quotations in a book review.

For more information, address:

TheGovernorsMen@outlook.com

First paperback edition May 2021

Cover design by David J. Hamilton

THE RESURGENCE

Book 2 of The Governor's Men

BY DAVID J. HAMILTON

1st Edition

Foreword

Firstly, my sincere thanks to you - the intrepid reader! If you're reading this, the odds are you've already struggled through my first book, 'The Administration', in what is intended to be a sci-fi trilogy. You will therefore be familiar with the two main characters, the brothers Vil and Cassus, both of whom appear in this, the second book of the trilogy. If you have not had the misfortune to read the Administration yet, it's available for a couple of quid online and will help to set the scene for this book: Its older, better and far more experienced brother. However, I should forewarn you that a considerable span of time separate the date when the first book was written and the release of its successor. I am told by my kinder friends that the Resurgence is the superior effort. It can certainly be read as a standalone novel.

I have taken several liberties with the second book in the Governor's men trilogy, most notably with respect to space travel. Readers with rapier like intellects have already pointed out the occasional flaws found here and I must state for the record that any mistakes made are entirely my own. I've deliberately twisted or ignored science to better fit my story, which is not only a poor allegory for the death of the age of reason but it is worth taking a moment here, at the outset, to think about the reality of space travel and just how overwhelming a concept it really is. Daunting for the incredibly talented and brave astronauts of the 1960's and early 70's and almost as daunting today, when the phone in your pocket is easily a million times more powerful than the guidance computer in Apollo 11 (I know I am prone to exaggerating, but in this instance, I am not). This remarkable computer for the time actually crashed on a number of occasions including, helpfully, during the descent of the 'Eagle' module to the moon in 1969. Imagine that if you will. Luckily, Armstrong possessed gigantic balls of the purest shining steel and was able to manually fly the lunar module parallel to the ground and land safely in the Sea of Tranquillity.

No human has visited the moon even within my immense life span, despite its relative proximity. Our satellite is on average 238,855 miles away from the Earth. 'That's a fair drive Dave', you might say and so it is. However, the nearest *stars* to Earth are in the Alpha Centauri triple-star system, which is about 4.37 light-years away. Proxima Centauri sits slightly closer, at 4.24 light-years. Let's call it 4.3 light-years though, because what's half a light year between friends. This equates to about 25 trillion miles (1 light year = 5.88 trillion miles). To put that in perspective, in some 296,000 years, Voyager 2 will pass 4.3 light-years from Sirius, the brightest star in the sky. *296,000 years*. And the Voyagers were launched in 1977 (a fantastic year all round). Voyager 1 eventually managed to limp out of our own solar system in 2012.

I have included a number of spaceships in this book, and refer repeatedly to hypersonic flight. As every schoolboy from the last century knows, typically we measure the speed of an aircraft by its Mach number, which is a velocity relative to the speed of sound (approximately 770 mph). Mach 1 is of course the speed of sound.

A *hypersonic vehicle* is one that can fly at over Mach 5. The X15 experimental test plane, also from the 1960's, is one such machine. A machine piloted on occasion by Neil Armstrong himself. This 'space plane' could reach a speed of over 4,500 mph.

The heat exchange engines described in this novel are based on Reaction Engines SABRE rocket engine. This is a genuine UK engineering project as opposed to a made up one. Rest assured though that in the finest British tradition, this great work will be sold off as soon as it becomes commercially viable to the Americans, the Germans, the Indians, the Chinese or indeed anyone who asks. Your mum could probably buy it. In exchange the UK will receive a packet of beans, some shiny buttons and legions of half-baked promises about keeping employment (of cats) in the UK for at least 2 weeks after point of sale. But I digress! An engine like this is reported to be capable of speeds of Mach 25 outside of orbit. I have taken the liberty of improving this statistic rather significantly. Without mentioning specifics and for argument's sake, let us take a hypothetical speed of Mach 100 or 76,700 miles per hour (21 miles per second). To travel but 1 light year at this speed would still take over 8,500 years! If I left this year, I'd be less than a quarter of the distance to Proxima Centauri in the 106th century AD (or CE for you 19th century buffs you!) Even with stasis over several or even dozens of years, this is well beyond the human life span, Yoda's life span and probably the endurance of both species, homo sapiens and er, Yoda or even baby Yoda.

Given the problem this would pose for a mediocre writer of fiction such as myself, I have therefore *simply ignored* the reality of the incredible distances involved in space travel whilst still trying to convey the extremities of distance involved, even with the future technology available to my characters. In Chapter 1 of The Administration, I refer to the break-through in inter-stellar travel in the late 21st century, but did not specify what that may be. I have intentionally steered away (no pun intended) from FTL (faster than light) drives. Research into Warp drives has continued in patches over the last 20 years but remains largely theoretical. The literature cites 'insurmountable obstacles' to break through to deliver a working FTL drive. Although the principles are rather different, it's still worth noting that 100 years ago men had only been flying under power for 17 years, so who knows where we will be in another decade, let alone another century.

On a personal note, I still believe in the scientific method and progress, despite the many problems the West is currently facing. We find ourselves in a peculiar time, when genuine hardship has been forgotten for many and trivial problems are then conflated into mythic proportions. Perpetual victimhood status has somehow become acceptable and indeed holds sway over public discourse and ludicrously, people's 'feelings' are permitted to eclipse that most valuable of commodities - the truth. Real values, merit and worth are being replaced at the insistence of the permanently outraged. These people are fantastic at tearing things down and re-writing or even erasing history and seem to expend an awful lot of energy doing so, but they rarely create or add to the sum of our knowledge as a species or try to solve anything. Yet beneath this thick crust of ignorance, there are reasons to be positive. Not least amongst these the tremendous work by a growing raft of private companies which simply did not exist even when I wrote the first book and like the space-race of the 1960's, there's a new and exciting technological 'race' to put humans back in deep space within a few hand-span of years. One of the most recent steps being the landing of NASA's *Perseverance* Rover on Mars after a seven-month space flight. Part of the mission brief for this remarkable machine being to prepare for the arrival of humans at some future date. Maybe these endeavours will provide a suitable stimulus for people to start looking up to the stars once again and reignite the raw indomitable spirit of mankind.

I have added a few appendices to this book to provide some 'behind the scenes' detail. This includes a section on the Perga, a ship which features prominently in this story, a full list of her crew and some brief character biographies.

CHAPTER 1

CHAPTER 2

CHAPTER 3

CHAPTER 4

CHAPTER 5

CHAPTER 6

CHAPTER 7

CHAPTER 8

CHAPTER 9

CHAPTER 10

CHAPTER 11

CHAPTER 12

CHAPTER 13

CHAPTER 14

CHAPTER 15

APPENDICES

Full List of Appendices:

The crew of the Perga
Main character biographies
List of Central Computer Department (CCD) Regulators
Influential Actavian Senators
Selected Section Heads (& Equivalent)
The Perga
Ranks of the Actavian Defence Force
Ranks of the Toradon Navy

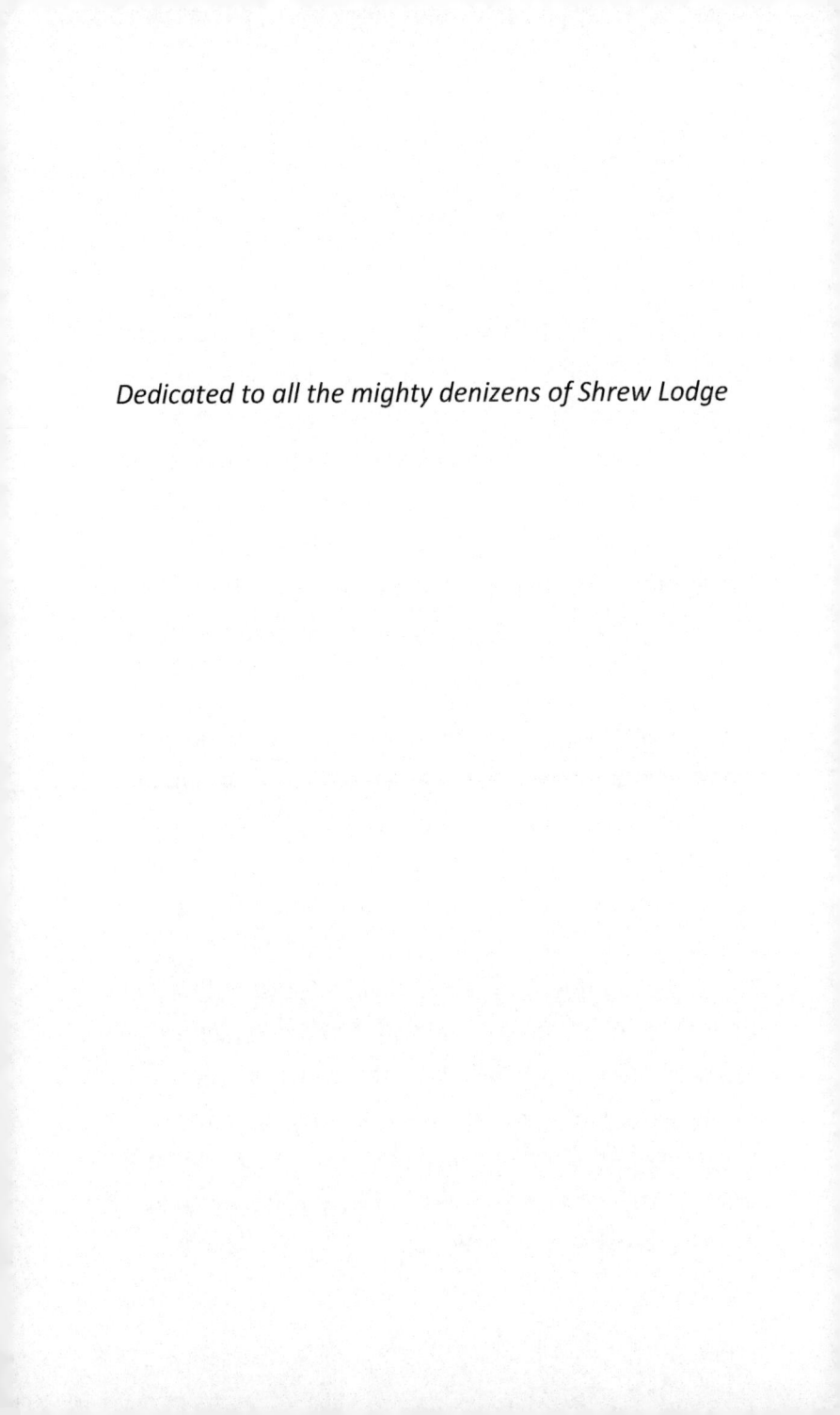

Dedicated to all the mighty denizens of Shrew Lodge

CHAPTER 1

Almost ten years had passed since the coup. Cassus gazed out of the Senate house veranda at the city below. 'Governor' Cassus now he thought, for the umpteenth time. The great square was surrounded with completed developments and bustling with life. EV's and great tubular public transmods flowed into the central terminus taking people to and from the new city, now known as Novum Civitas or just 'Novum', back to the original colony settlement of Acto and beyond.

Monumental buildings in a harmonious fusion of classical and modern Actavian architecture spread out from the vast square below. No longer comprised of half completed facades or a veneer of development but fully functioning occupied buildings filled with the highly skilled workforce of Acto, all contributing to the thriving economy. To the south were located the brand-new space ports linking the planet to the Planetary Network, amongst which Acto had grown considerably in power and influence over the last decade. The proximity of the major space ports to the monumental city was there to remind all planetary visitors of Acto's growing prestige and power.

Dozens of light launch vehicles flitted to and from the passenger cruisers above the atmosphere, transporting thousands of people to other major systems on a daily basis. A grand row of statues lined the path to the Senate House, memorialising the heroes of what had become known as the Toradon revolution. The pioneer erected by Governor Sendrick remained in situ but had been joined by statues of Sergeant Barthan, Corporal Rhodes and Vil Toradon. These stood, amongst others, facing the Senate and marbled colossal statues of the twin saviours of Acto, Governor Cassus and Captain Coldor. The behemoths stood flanking the Senate doors – Great Patrician visages frozen in paternal benevolence, eyes regarding the heavens, left arms raised in benediction, pointing out towards the heroes and beyond to the Core (the city of Acto). The fingers on the right hand of the statue of Cassus were held aloft but spread symbolising the five main settlements of Acto, each fingertip glowing gently in a warm golden light. There was a common rumour amongst the citizenry that if ever one of the cities was under attack or suffered from some natural disaster the corresponding finger would glow red.

Cassus sighed quietly and headed back inside, the automated double doors gliding silently closed behind him. Immediately, several aides swarmed towards him, loaded with data pads and a seemingly never-ending amount of electronic paperwork that needed his attention. Cassus batted them away with barely concealed irritation. Only a few weeks remained before the tenth anniversary of freedom from the tyranny of the previous central Administration and apparently there were a thousand tiny details that needed his attention. Cassus didn't much care what colour the smoke from the Actavian Space-force fly-by was and had mixed feelings towards the celebrations in general but that he supposed was the price that he had to pay as liberator and Governor. However, after weeks of accepting the inevitable Cassus had had enough of his own bureaucracy and had decided to reward himself with a day off; even if he hadn't told most of his Council or the Senators. He wished for a moment that Coldor was still on-planet as the two had grown closer in the aftermath of the revolution and the frantic days of rebuilding but Coldor had finally left three years ago for the frontier planet *7800-444*, known locally as the 'Garden' which was ironic as the planet was a rock. Dead and unforgiving, albeit rich in mineral wealth.

Cassus hurtled past the Planning department, picking up speed as he fled. He spied Octavia Brinsmead, now the Head of Acto's Planet Planning and Development

(APPD) looking at plans in her glass box office as he slipped past.

He made it to the rear service stairs and took the stairs two at a time down to a rear basement loading bay and a waiting outbound Electronic Vehicle (OEV) which was linked to his personal device and had already powered up. Cassus jumped in the driver's side and swiftly disabled the automatic driver. The need to get away was building to a crescendo. He was about to reverse when his body guard flung himself into the passenger seat, causing the EV to wobble alarmingly.

"Hey! You surely weren't thinking of going somewhere without me?" asked Brox. "I'm beyond hurt beyond belief!"

"Damn it Brox! You're like a second shadow."

"That's what you pay me for," Brox shrugged.

"Come on. Let's get out of here before the Senate can think of a reason to keep me stuffed up in my office like some sort of curiosity."

"All set boss. So, where we going anyway?"

Cassus glanced at Brox, whose muscular bulk filled the passenger side of the cab. His elite purple guard uniform stretched skin-tight against his powerful torso.

Despite his size, he didn't loom over Cassus, if anything he looked a little comical as he sat hunched up into his seat. Cassus knew his demeanour was affected though. He'd seen Brox in action from a shortlist of Actavian Guardsmen who'd all excelled at physical combat. Strip aside the self-depreciation, humour and occasional cheek (sometimes more than occasional) and Cassus had no doubt that his guard and friend was a lethal human weapon.

"We're off to frontier town Broxy boy; Star city," Cassus grunted and started the vehicle. The EV ascended quietly up the lightweight steel mesh ramp and the double doors slid smoothly open. Cassus spun the wheel aggressively, palming the vehicle around a corner and away from the Senate. Within minutes they were out of the new city outskirts and onto wide open road that threaded its way past rock and red dust like a black snake. Cassus grinned and jammed his foot down hard on the accelerator.

*****

Star City was a founded during the last Administration when Cassus and his brother Vil were both still children.

It was over forty miles from the Core at Acto and even further from Novum. The new road from Novum was a recent addition pushed through the Senate by Cassus himself.

To Cassus's slight embarrassment and secret pleasure, it had been named the 'Governor's Boulevard'.

"What's it like driving on your own road chief?" Brox enquired.

Cassus raised one eyebrow, "Pretty much the same as any other road I'm guessing," he said sardonically.

"They're *all* my roads though," he added deadpan.

Brox shot him a look. For a moment a barb of anxiety gripped him. He liked joking with Cassus. He knew there was a growing bond of friendship, but there was a limit to how much he could antagonize the most powerful man on the planet. Then he saw the slight curl of Cassus's lip and laughed. "You almost had me there! I was about to have a heart attack." he quipped, holding his chest with both massive hands.

"That'll teach you," said Cassus who chuckled briefly.

They drove in companionable silence for several minutes.

"What's happening at Star City then that's so urgent? You don't normally visit this time of the week," Brox said, squirming in his seat to get comfortable.

Cassus was quiet for a few moments. "I just needed to get away for a couple of hours Brox. That and the fact that the first deep space mission we've launched for thirty years is only a month away from launch.

*****

The Star City dome appeared on the horizon. The tech hub and launch facilities had nearly doubled in size since its inception. New 3D printed buildings spread out from the upgraded control tower at the dome's heart. Various sub-orbital launch pads for logistical support surrounded the dome. The Boulevard ended in a wide asphalted area fronting a multiple bay delivery warehouse and EV parking. Beyond the dome stood the Thirty-mile tower, known colloquially, even affectionately, as the *Space Pencil*. The extreme height, high tensile structure, rose up and up into the atmosphere. Built from 3D printed diamond weave Nano-thread directly onto the old rocket launch pad, the tower was fixed to dozens of foundations buried deep in Acto's mantle and the Star City dome itself. A high-level walkway connected the apex of the dome to the passenger lounge that sat two hundred and fifty feet above the ground on top of warehousing space below. The space pencil was Acto's solution to delivering cheap deep space exploration. The launch zone sat above the planetary atmosphere which enabled efficient ship launches without hugely wasteful rocket propulsion or the *ground to orbit* heat exchange engines upon which most of the colonised planets within the Planetary Network relied.

The Governor's Boulevard connected up the old road network and linked up each component part of the complex. Cassus viewed it with a mild sense of paternal pride. Ultra-modern construction techniques linked with ancient theory made possible by Acto's growing wealth and forward thinking. Of all the colonised planets only the mother planet and the droid planet Trestel had similar mega structures although most of the older colonies used launch facilities in the exosphere above their planetary atmospheres to reduce launch costs.

Cassus eased the OEV precisely into a parking bay and powered down. The pressurized doors hissed open and he and his burly passenger climbed out.

"I've seen the 'pencil two dozen times now but it still gets me every time," said Brox, staring up past the dome into the sky.

Cassus joined him and together the two men stood for a few moments to look at the endless tower disappear high above like a shining rope dropped from heaven.

*****

"Hello Vil! Guess who?" said Cassus.

Vil stopped in mid-stride and spun round. "Well, well, well, could it be that erstwhile brother of mine - The Governor! The Governor I say! To what do we owe this pleasure?"

"Do I need an excuse to keep an eye on this Administration's most expensive project?

"You're always welcome here Cassus. Just don't touch anything."

Fine, fine. I won't press any of these tempting green buttons," Cassus responded in good humour. "Not disturbing you, am I?"

"Not at all. I was just on my way over to the old labs to check on FJ."

"Ah, I see." Cassus's smile retreated slightly and his brow creased.

"How is the old loony?"

Vil had watched his brother intently and noted his expression. "Much the same as ever. His mind is still razor sharp. To be honest, this close to launch he is almost unbearable." Vil hesitated. "He still blames himself. About what happened."

"It wasn't his fault," Cassus said automatically. "Governor Sendrick's predecessor, Governor Cole, gave the order."

"That's true Cassus. So just don't go into Governor mode or give him a hard a time."

Cassus grunted and set off, striding down familiar corridors to the old lab buildings where his parents had once worked. Vil glanced at Brox who shrugged and they hurried to catch up with their leader, brother, friend.

*****

Cassus stopped at the sealed entrance and engaged the retina scan.

"Entry granted. Welcome Governor Toradon."

Cassus stepped briskly into the lab.

"Who's that?" A sharp, precise voice came from behind a workstation. "I asked not to be disturbed at this critical juncture! I will be having words with young Toradon again later." Frederick Jasper adjusted a control on his multi-screen dashboard and finally peered around.

"Hello FJ. You'll just have to make do with the older Toradon instead."

"Governor!" FJ squawked. "I'm sorry, I didn't know. You haven't cleared ... I mean, I wasn't informed..." the old scientist tailed off. A series of emotions fleetingly etched on his face. Shock quickly followed by confusion; a fleeting trace of guilt.

Cassus just watched him quietly. Impassive.

Moments later Vil and Brox cleared the security check and entered the lab behind Cassus.

"You remembered the way then?"

"Not likely to forget Vil. We used to play here every weekend."

Vil could see the creeping onset of one of his brother's darker moods. The crease in his forehead, the cold stare and slight lean forward into a more aggressive stance. They were becoming more common as the weight of leadership took its toll. Vil racked his brains for something to jolt Cassus's state of mind.

"Remember when we got caught breaking into the 'Ellipse' before the test launch? I thought Dad was going to throttle you!"

Cassus cast his mind back thirty or so years to the day when as a boisterous 12-year-old he and his 9-year-old brother had snuck out a classroom in the lab complex with a security access card purloined from their Mum's bag. Avoiding the perimeter guard, they'd caught the elevator to the deep space exploration ship 'Ellipse', which was scheduled to blast off later that week with their parents at the helm. Vil and Cassus had been found on the flight deck sitting in their parents' flight seats, wearing their anti-glare headsets pretending to be space adventurers.

It was the one of the few times that Cassus could remember his father being angry and one of the last vivid memories he had of him. Despite the explosion of anger from both their parents he knew, even then, that beneath the scolding there was a certain pride. Cassus had seen the twinkle in his Father's eye as he'd hoisted him bodily out of the ship and back to ground level. He had been shaking his head at the audacity of it. Their mother had lectured him sternly and extensively on taking responsibility for his actions and setting an example, but he'd overheard them later chuckling quietly together. His Mother had said something about boys being boys. They'd sounded happy and sad at the same time.

A week later his parents had blasted off on Acto's last great exploration of the frontier. Neither he nor Vil ever saw them again in the flesh.

Cassus bent his head but these were old memories, turned over a thousand times in his head over more than a quarter of a century. The pain was old and manageable.

"I seem to recall they weren't best pleased. Naturally, I blamed you Vil. Always getting me into trouble!"

"What! I was about five years old," Vil gasped indignantly, nonetheless pleased to be back on familiar ground.

"You were nine actually," FJ corrected him.

Cassus gave a short bark of laughter but his eyes creased and his mood was lifted.

"Let's have an update then please FJ" he instructed.

*****

The veteran scientist provided the Governor with a succinct account of the latest developments in readiness for launch in two weeks.

"Has the shielding process of the beta voltaic nuclear batteries been completed?" asked Vil.

"The portable double skin shielding was installed yesterday," FJ confirmed, nodding. "Each is running at optimal capacity and should last for around a hundred years or so. Maybe a little less."

"Excellent. How many will be ready in time for launch?" Asked Cassus.

FJ puffed up with pride. "The full complement of four batteries are ready to be shipped Governor."

"Er, wait a minute, did you say 'nuclear batteries'? Are those things safe?" Asked Brox.

FJ pointed a long, thin finger right in his face, almost touching the big man's nose. "Look Pox; This is 21st century technology. They are quite, quite safe."

Brox muttered, "it's Brox, not Pox", and crossed his arms. He continued to look sceptical.

"Just don't drop one," Vil added helpfully.

"Not Ever."

"Shall we take a look then?"

FJ looked aghast. "At the batteries?""

"No, I don't need to see the batteries FJ. If you say they are ready, then they are ready."" Said Cassus gently.

"I'm talking about the ship. The Perga. Let's take a peek."

"But we haven't had any notice!" FJ gasped, flummoxed. "I'll have to clear it with control, prepare the suits, the elevator!" FJ exclaimed, waving a data pad erratically at Cassus. "You can't just 'peek' at it! It's sitting 30 miles directly above us," the data pad waved in the air alarmingly close to the Governor's face, "You and the team weren't scheduled to undertake your first pre-flight inspection until next week!"

"No time like the present FJ. I've got all day you know. Now make the arrangements please!" Cassus shooed the frenetic scientist away.

Dismissed, FJ scuttled off grumbling loudly about schedules and certain precocious Governors. Cassus turned to Vil and Brox, "Shall we retire to departure lounge then gentlemen. I want to take a look at this ship of ours."

CHAPTER 2

Cassus, Vil and Brox settled down in a sparsely decorated lounge that formed part of a suite of rooms at the top of the Dome. This attached to the passage that led directly to the space pencil for passengers and flight crew. Brox gazed out of the floor to ceiling window and nibbled on a protein bar as Cassus and Vil sat on two plastic chairs and conversed quietly.

Within a few minutes two technicians bustled past and hastily saluted Cassus who returned the salute. The technicians were followed by another familiar face.

"Lucinda!" Vil almost yelled. He ran over and hugged her tight.

Lucinda squeezed Vil back, "It's nice to see you too Vil but would you mind letting me breathe again in a minute please?"

"Oh, yes of course," said Vil releasing the whip-thin frame of Lucinda from his grasp.

"I see you haven't forgotten me then?" Lucinda Grey beamed back at him.

"As if I could ever forget you Lucinda."

"Well, I suppose I am rather unforgettable," Lucinda remarked flatly.

Vil and Lucinda had both been victims of the previous Administration's conscription raids and forced into hard labour before Cassus, then an assistant to Governor Sendrick, had raised a small force and rescued them from Novum city on the eve of the Governor's triumphal speech. The shared experience had forged a bond between them that had endured over the next ten years. For nine of those years Lucinda had run the hydroponic production Domes over at Acto's second and most northerly settlement of City-gens. For the last half-year Lucinda and her number two, Hamilton Lamb, had assisted Vil in preparing the Perga for its first expeditionary run. Lamb was to join the crew and run the ship's Hydroponics section and Lucinda would return to head up food production at City-gens.

Behind her stood the short but commanding figure of Elara Blanc, adjutant to Vil at Star City and safety officer for the whole compound.

"I hear someone has ordered an unscheduled visit to the Perga?" Elara said, looking between Vil and Cassus. Vil shrugged and tipped his head towards his brother. Cassus just nodded.

"Fine by me Governor. I'll just give you all a quick safety briefing and refresh on emergency procedures and get you suited up. Then we'll head over to the pencil by way of the dome pass. It's a short walk so we'll be aboard the Perga in just over an hour. This way please."

Cassis, Vil, Brox and Lucinda followed Elara into a large adjoining room. There were rows of tall lockers against three of the walls and a double row of wide benches against the gentle curve of the Dome which formed the outer wall and window of the room. A number of different types of suit were available including the Z81 Extravehicular activity (EVA) suit and the light weight Acto Stargazer 1500 intravehicular activity (IVA) suits.

"IVA suits everyone," Elara directed.

"The vermillion coloured ones Brox," said Vil.

"Those are the red ones" Lucinda chipped in helpfully.

"I know that!" Brox scowled.

Vil and Lucinda had more experience with suiting up than Cassus and Brox and methodically pulled their suits on whilst Elara helped Cassus and Brox into theirs.

"I haven't done this for a while," Cassus admitted.

"You should have come to more training sessions!"

Elara admonished. "It will soon come flooding back though Governor," she added as an emollient.

As soon as everyone was suited up, Elara directed them to the benches and prepared them for the elevation to the waiting ship. Fifteen minutes later and the briefing had been concluded.

"That's it everyone. Now grab your helmets and follow me."

Elara led them back to the lounge and though to a heavy shutter in the far wall which opened automatically. Intermittent recessed red strip LED's provided a weak light in the dome pass. The transfer passage was fully enclosed and gloomy. The five travellers walked quietly in the semi-darkness, boots echoing on the bare metal grill floor, shadows flickering black and red against clammy skin. The temperature was uncomfortable, the heat pricked against skin.

Cassus looked around at his companions. Vil was contemplative, his mind elsewhere, Lucinda looked determined and Brox looked sticky. Sweat glistened on his dark skin, his eyes flitting everywhere.

"You alright Brox? Cassus asked.

Brox swung his head round jerkily, "Is it me or is too warm in here. Where's the comfort cooling at? I thought this compound was supposed to be cutting edge?" Brox grinned dutifully, but the smile didn't quite reach his eyes.

"Almost there now. Just a quick trip up the elevator and we'll be aboard the Perga."

Brox nodded noncommittally. Shortly afterwards they reached the passenger departure elevator lounge which was little more than a large holding area with several supply lockers and security checkpoints; currently unmanned. Elara manipulated the controls on a standalone console to one side of the reinforced doors that were arranged over two storeys. A simple staircase led up to a mezzanine for access to the upper set of doors.

The pencil actually had four elevators, one for every side of the structure. Two cargo platforms and two dual level passenger lifts. These could be latched onto a super-steel ring shaped like a donut and revolved around the core of the pencil to the passenger or cargo launch bays.

"Helmets on gentlemen," Elara ordered.

"Yes Ma'am," said Brox.

"It's a pressurised cabin El," Vil protested "Do we really need to suit up?"

"It's a small box that takes us into space. I'm not taking any chances with the Governor here. It's my job to ensure his safety whilst off-planet," Elara said with a quick glance at Brox. "Yours too for that matter Vil." She squeezed Vil's arm briefly. "Count yourself lucky I am not insisting on an independent suit O2 supply as well."

"I'll take that as a yes," grumbled Vil as put his helmet on and sealed it.

"Test comms please" said Elara, tapping the side of her own helmet.

"Cassus reporting in."

"Brox in."

"Lucinda in."

"It's making my head hot," said Vil

Brox snorted and Cassus gave a short laugh from inside his helmet.

"Better to have a hot head than an exploded head" Lucinda advised wisely.

"Alright you lot. We're ready to embark. Let's get up there!" and without waiting Cassus engaged the heavy-duty manual lever to open the lower level doors and stepped through.

Vil, Lucinda and Elara quickly followed. Brox paused, took a deep breath, rolled his heavy shoulders and followed the Governor.

*****

The interior of the lift was painted in utilitarian black with exposed sections of dull leaden steel. A double green lighting strip ran continuously around the circumference of the lift above head height. Each level of the lift could seat eight people. Two flight grade chairs to a side faced inwards around a central console. Cargo nets hung from the walls on three sides behind the chairs. Oxygen tanks were built into the backs of the chairs and under the floor. An emergency hatch in the ceiling connected the two levels of the lift. The lift smelt vaguely of oil and machinery.

"Well, this is rudimentary," Lucinda noted.

"Only the finest of furnishings are good enough for our Governor," Vil quipped.

"How long will it take to get to the ship?" Brox asked, strapping himself in.

"About thirty minutes," Elara confirmed. "We can achieve higher velocities but I'm not aiming to break any records," she said looking at Cassus questioningly.

Cassus gave her the thumbs up as he settled himself into his flight seat.

"Who's done this trip before then?" asked Brox

"Vil and Lucinda have been up before" responded Elara, pointing vaguely at Vil, "and I've run at least two dozen trips now. You're quite safe big man."

"Ha! As if *I'm* worried," Brox scoffed.

Elara smiled in her helmet and shook her head slightly. After confirming the passengers were all strapped in, she engaged a control on the arm rest of her chair and a wafer-thin pad attached by a sucker to a flexible stalk extended towards her. Elara grabbed the pad. "Commencing initiation. Control, this is Commander Elara Blanc. Seeking clearance to embark."

There was a short pause. "This is control, copy that Commander. You are cleared for travel. Proceed at will and safe journey."

"Roger that control. Over and out."

"Get ready everyone – This is it!" Elara flicked open the activation control and pulled the lever. The lift vibrated noticeably and then shot upwards into the sky.

*****

"Sheesh! This thing is fast!" Brox gushed, holding on tight to the grips on the side of his flight chair, knuckles white under his flight suit.

Cassus said "Is it supposed to feel like this?" through gritted teeth.

"The first run is always the worst" Vil answered. "You get used to it by the third or fourth time."

"There isn't going to be a third or fourth time." Cassus promised as the huge lift continued its ascent into the heavens. Vil, Elara and Lucinda more or less relaxed, Cassus and Brox hanging on tightly.

"This is exhausting Elara, what's our ETA?"

"We're just passing the counterweight mechanism. About another five minutes to the docking station."

"Do they have any gin?" Lucinda asked hopefully.

Vil was about to reply when there a thunderous metallic clang on one side of the lift, startling everyone. The lights dimmed briefly.

"What was that?" Brox yelled.

Elara calmed the team whilst quickly scanning the instruments on her data pad. "Don't worry - There's no breach; no danger. We talked about this in the briefing. It was probably just a small meteorite. These passenger lifts are triple honeycomb skinned and can withstand huge pressure per square foot. We'll be fine."

"Well, this really is much more fun than normal!" Lucinda said, which brought smiles to the rest of the group.

A minute later the lift started to deaccelerate as it eased towards the docking station next to the Perga.

Cassus forced his shoulders to relax and cricked his neck left and right. As soon as the lights on the central console turned to green, he unstrapped himself and without waiting for Elara strode towards the airlock door.

*****

The space station attached to the top of the elevator was shaped like a small wheel. It was tiny in comparison to the Star City compound. The wheel rotated quickly in order to enough to generate a sufficient artificial gravity through a centrifugal force. Cassus bounded in and cast his eye around until he found what he was looking for. A steep bare metal staircase leading up to a gallery. Without waiting for the others, he negotiated his way through the cramped station and with an increasing sense of urgency up the stairs to the 360-degree viewing gallery above.

Whipping his helmet off, he finally cast his eyes on the ship that was to take him and his crew to the frontier.

The Perga.

At almost 3,500 feet in length, the sleek shaft of the ship had two rotating rings at either end, the first sitting behind the bridge of the ship, the second sitting two thirds down the length of the vessel in front of the huge deployable solar sail. The stern of the ship was dedicated to the bank of four powerful heat-exchange *Panther* class engines sitting in a square, two by two. The whole ship gave the appearance of being poised, capable. It demanded respect.

"Fuck me," said Cassus quietly as he gazed at it.

Cassus was joined by Vil, then Brox and Lucinda and lastly Elara. They stood side by side and stared out into the infinite star-scape, the Perga sat leashed, surrounded by inky blackness and a million points of light. Behind the Perga sat the bare bones of her, as yet unnamed, sister ship. A dark hulk next to the radiance of the completed vessel. Cassus swallowed and clenched his fists. He was the Governor of one of the mankind's most successful colonies, a great man. Perhaps. Still just a spec in time against the vastness of the cosmos.

Brox whistled. "That's some ship."

"It should be," said Vil, "it cost enough."

"It was time. Too long have we dallied in the Federation. Apart from the 'Garden' when was the last time the Planetary Network founded a new colony?" asked Lucinda.

Vil thought for a moment, "Must be about twenty years."

"Nearer to thirty" Cassus confirmed, "and you're absolutely right Luce – This is our time. Come on, let's have a look inside. Elara, can you do the honours please."

Elara snapped to attention and saluted, closely followed by Brox. The solemnity of the moment seemed to call for it.

"It will be my pleasure Governor."

Minutes later the hatch to the Perga's inbound crew chamber hissed open. Elara stood aside and gestured for Cassus to enter.

Cassus gave her a quick smile and stepped aboard his ship for the first time, closely followed by Brox and Lucinda. Vil shot a quick look at Elara, who smiled back.

"Let's just hope it lives up to his expectations," Vil remarked quietly.

*****

Cassus stepped through the hatch and looked around. He had memorized the layout of the vessel over many hours poring over the schematics and holo-models of the ship. The main contractor had even presented him with an actual scale model of the Perga, which sat on his desk. So much work over the years had led up to this moment and now he was finally aboard. He reached out to touch the ship and overhead the lights winked on one after another.

"At last," he said softly. "Not long now," and turned to the others, some of whom would be crew members with him on the voyage.

"Better in real life huh?" said Vil. The whole crew, including Cassus, had run dozens of training exercises in a mock-up of the critical parts of the ship back in Star City. "What would you like to see first?" asked Vil.

"It's a shame I don't have time for a full tour today. The Administration will be wondering where I am, but at the very least I'd like to see the bridge, the hibernation capsules and the droid complement. The rest can wait until launch day," Cassus answered.

Brox looked guilty. "They know where you are sir. You've turned off all your comms but I've kept Commander Hill advised of our progress."

Cassus raised an eyebrow. "I should have known. Thought it was suspiciously quiet! Come on, I want to see the bridge".

The bridge was one of the largest spaces aboard the ship by virtue of so many of the crew spending a large part of their duty time there. A number of stations were clustered around the convex forward screen including the weapons control, science, communications, navigation and droid systems as well as the Captain's command chair set further back. To the rear there was a briefing room, a refresh station with a few additional seats for visiting passengers, a tiny washroom and a large locker bay with emergency equipment and suits. A hatch in the floor led to a secure compact emergency bridge and a bank of four escape pods which were also accessible from the two levels below them.

"What do you think chief?" asked Lucinda as Elara showed Brox the weapon station and Vil fiddled with a heads-up display.

"It's difficult to comprehend Lucinda. I'm still getting to grips with it. So far though, I couldn't have asked for more."

"Everyone, get over here!" With some difficulty Vil shooed Brox and Elara back to Cassus and Lucinda. Vil addressed the ship's primary computer, "Exa, take a pic. Say cheese everyone!"

"Photograph logged Vil" Exa confirmed and a giant digital image popped onto the main forward viewscreen.

"Cassus, you're not smiling!" Vil accused.

"No. I didn't even say cheese," Cassus responded.

The group made their way to the next level down where the hibernation capsules were located, close to the bridge and adjacent to the medical and recreation facilities.

The Perga's shared stasis chamber could accommodate fifty crew members at a time. The Perga itself could comfortably accommodate almost one-hundred and fifty people but could function with a skeleton crew of three. Cassus had almost forty volunteers for the outbound mission. Once sleep had been induced, the stasis chamber worked by slowly cooling its occupants' body temperature to around 32C, lowering blood pressure and slowing the heart considerably. The chamber induced relatively short cycles of crew members going in and out of stasis, monitored at all times by one of the on-duty crew members. The stasis cycle could run for up to a month with the ship's artificial gravity and electrical stimulation maintaining healthy muscle mass.

Vil proudly pointed out how the communal system operated "It's so much more efficient and lighter than the personal stasis pods on the old Colony ships and today's cruisers. We've been able to dedicate the space saved to the rec-facs instead."

"He means recreational facilities" Lucinda advised as she caught Cassus looking puzzled.

Elara frowned, "Can't say I'm especially eager to get into stasis." Brox nodded in agreement. "This facility is safe isn't it?"

"Perfectly safe El" said Vil a little defensively. It's been tested extensively. I did a stint for almost a week and look at me."

"That's ... Exactly my point!" Elara winked.

"As long as they don't pipe those damn self-improvement lessons into my brain, I can live with it"

"Don't worry Brox. There's no subliminal messages on this facility," Vil assured him but as soon as Brox has turned away he mouthed 'There are' to Lucinda who raised an eyebrow and tried unsuccessfully not to giggle.

"What?" Brox asked. "What is it?" to no response.

The rest of the tour passed quickly. Brox lingered in the armoury whilst Cassus and Elara inspected the ships complement of droids. These were sixty multi-role RDG class humanoid droids currently folded into storage position in three rows of ten on either side of a central gantry and one RDX class humanoid master droid that stood immobile in front of a control console at the end of the room. It had a lightweight but durable flexible polymer skin and whilst it was distinctly droid like, its shape was definitely female.

Elara made a face. "Ugh. These things are creepy. You sure you want to take a droid army with you Governor?"

Cassus tore his gaze from the RDX. "It's hardly an army Elara and yes, I've been over this many times. I have a feeling these things could come in handy."

"Acto has never been dependent on droid-tech before though. We had to import these from the planet Trestel."

"I know, but I want every tool at my disposal and these are cutting edge. You know how many operational RDX class droid there are?"

"Maybe a dozen or so?"

"Three. That includes this one." Cassus pondered, "I should give her a name I suppose."

Elara snorted. "Her? Come on Governor – We need to head back to the surface. The Administration will have my head if I don't get you back safely soon."

Cassus nodded absently. "Are you ready for this Elara? We will be away from home for several months, possibly longer."

Elara looked up at Cassus, who stood ramrod straight, broad shoulders imposing in the confined space. His eyes bore into hers and her neck tingled. She realized how closely they were standing and wondered how that had happened. Her lips parted slightly. "I ... I am Governor."

"Call me Cassus please, no need for formality here."

"Yes Cassus. I have prepared for this for years." Elara paused, "and sacrificed much to be here."

"You certainly have Elara." Cassus said gently. "You are a true pioneer; a fine Actavian and a fine woman." Cassus gripped her shoulder firmly for a moment and then stepped quickly past her.

"Come on El! You'll make me late." He said over his shoulder.

Elara looked down at her hand which she has instinctively rested on the shoulder Cassus had touched.

"I'm coming Cassus," she said, but too softly for him to hear.

*****

Within ten minutes the team had reassembled by the outbound crew chamber. Cassus stood in front of the hatch, facing them.

"We're not due to depart for a month or so until after the celebrations but before we make the descent, I want to say a few words. I want to thank you all for your commitment and endeavours over the last few months and years to make this voyage a reality." One by one, Cassus looked all of them in the eye, "You have *all* made sacrifices. There is no doubt in my mind though that those sacrifices will be worth the price you've paid. You are making history. You will be remembered as such. You all share my view that mankind has now entered another age of stagnation. With the exception of colony 7800-400, the so called 'Garden' and some new asteroid mining operations, there hasn't been an outbound voyage for decades. Over two centuries of interstellar travel and we have still not encountered intelligent life. I intend to try and rectify that. Together, we will be the spark for the next generation of explorers, the catalyst that transforms the Federation of Planets into an outward looking force for expansion, for enlightenment and scientific progress, once again."

"You're damn right we are" Brox exclaimed, fist clenched amongst nods and affirmation from the others.

"Right, speech over," Cassus was breathing quickly. He glanced around again, a little self-consciously.

Elara's had no reservations, "Three cheers for Governor Cassus" and Brox roared mightily beside her as Vil and Lucinda added their voices to the sweet ovation. Cassus flushed red.

"You go on," he told them. "I just need a minute."

CHAPTER 3

Much later the next day after an uneventful descent to Star City and a morning spent calming irate Senators and Regulators, Cassus had retired to his office and locked the door. Brox lurked like a hulk outside as an extra deterrent to potential petitioners. Cassus had summoned Vil who sat in the deep green leather chair opposite, an equally deep frown on his face.

Cassus set his mouth in a hard line. "I'm sorry Vil, but you're not coming with me on this trip."

"You're joking? I've practically organised the whole thing! You can't just ditch me at the last moment. We're launching in a few weeks!"

"It's too risky. You know what happened to Mum and Dad. I will not lose you too. Anyway, I need someone to keep an eye on things here."

"That's not your choice to make Cassus!"

Cassus's eyes narrowed, "Fortunately for you, it is my choice as I am Governor here. Not you." Cassus saw his brother's frustration and disappointment and softened his tone, "Look it's not for long. I will be back before you know it."

"It's a whole year! Knowing you, I expect it could be longer."

"No time at all. I'm not asking Vil. You have a family here. Lucinda and many of our friends will still be here, not on the ship and besides, I need you to manage the CCD and the Senate for me. I can assure you; they will keep you fully occupied."

"I'm not even a Regulator Cassus! How am I supposed to step straight into your shoes?" Said Vil, frantically groping around in his head for arguments. "Besides, the Senate will never agree to it. There's no precedent for a sibling to take over the Governorship!"

"Vil, your wife is a Regulator, as is your old friend Alan Spartan. You've known most of the rest for a decade or more. I think you'll manage. If I had any doubt in my mind about your abilities, I would invest one of the other Regulators. The Senate's view is irrelevant. Your investiture is under executive order and besides it's time limited. Some of the Senators don't like it but you will have plenty of allies."

"What about that old fool Lyron. He can't like this"

Cassus sighed, "*Senator* Lyron will accept it as an executive order. All you need to do is keep things on an even keel whilst I'm gone." Cassus looked at Vil expectantly, "It will be much easier for you to do that if you don't antagonize the Senators. Especially Lyron."

Vil raised an eyebrow "I know that Cassus. I don't want to stir things up in your absence; I don't want the job in the first place." He pursed his lips and puffed out his breath in exasperation and stared hard at the floor. The moment stretched and stretched. Cassus tapped his fingers on his cushioned arm-rest and waited. Vil dragged his gaze up.

"Why me? Why not Perterson or Kathryn - They are both capable people."

"Immensely capable, but you know me better than that. Blood will out. I have trust in the Colonel and Kathryn but it's not absolute. What we have begun here," Cassus gestured around the office and the city behind him and pointed at Vil. "It cannot be allowed to fail before it has even begun. We are elevated up above all others because of a course of action that you started Vil. Now it is your time to step up."

Resigned, Vil closed his eyes and rubbed his temples, "I did and you're right. We cannot cast aside everything we have achieved." Vil grinned suddenly, "but don't expect your office to look the same when you get back. Honestly, the décor in here is remarkably bad!"

Cassus laughed with pleasure and no more small measure of relief. He hadn't fully known which way Vil would swing or how he would react. Vil's temper was rare but more unpredictable than his own. He extended his arm and gripped Vil's hand. "I could hardly ask you to accept the job without redecorating. Feel free to restock the bar whilst you're at it. See, there are some perks to the role. Now, we've settled that I need to introduce you formally to a couple of the Senators who will be witnessing your investiture. Just so you know, Senator Temorri and his aide-de-camp are accompanying me as representatives of the Senate on this voyage.

"Oh!" Vil bit back a retort with some difficulty. "Least that's one less for me to deal with."

Cassus rose and walked around the desk to stand behind Vil. He spoke into his sleeve comms unit. "Brox, you can let them in now."

"Roger that Governor. They've been waiting out here for a while. Lyron looks like he might have an apoplexy by the way."

"Send them in then". Cassus patted Vil's shoulder and stood, arms behind his back to welcome his guests.

The double doors on the eastern wall opened and Brox stepped through and saluted, all trace of humour absent from his face.

"Senators Sej Lyron and Gilberto Temorri, Governor, with aide-de-camp Dawn Haran." Brox announced at in stentorian tones.

Cassus beamed at his guests and bid them to sit in a small lounge area beside his desk. "Welcome senators and Miss Haran."

"It's *Ms* actually" Dawn uttered, her ponderous chubby face dripping disdain. Small, angry eyes darting around in perpetual disapproval of everything she could perceive and most that she couldn't.

Cassus raised an eyebrow a fraction, "Of course *Ms* Haran. I thought that form of address had died out on Earth over three centuries ago. Are you singlehandedly intent on resurrecting it to the Galaxy? How remarkable. You may refer to *me* as Governor. Or Sir."

Senator Temorri interrupted, gesturing in what he thought was a conciliatory manner. "Come, come. Come now, let's get down to business." The Senator was in later middle age, slightly rotund around the middle but not without strength in the chest and shoulders. He was almost completely bald but had a small, pepper-pot moustache which he often stroked with his index finger.

"We've been waiting for over fifteen minutes! Senator Lyron spat, eyes flashing. The senator was in his late forties and still slim and toned. His black hair was retreating into a widow's peak and shot through with bright silver. His white uniform slashed with purple trim which continued as a wide stripe down the trousers that in turn were tucked into soft black leather calf boots. He looked every inch the senator and bore himself with tremendous import.

Cassus regarded him coolly. "You're here now Senators." He indicated towards Vil. "You know my brother of course?"

Temorri nodded amiably, like a benevolent uncle. Lyron spared Vil a brief glance, "The senate is not universal in its approval of this investiture plan Governor. There's a real risk of political fall-out in your absence."

"Then it is lucky Vil will have you here to assist him with this temporary state of affairs Senator Lyron! I am delighted to advise you that he has accepted the role pro tem."

Lyron smiled thinly at Vil, "A great honour of course".

"One I am sure he will excel at. Vil's stewardship of my role will not apply to off-planet interests, which naturally include my captaincy of the Perga." Cassus reached out and lightly touched Senator Temorri on the upper arm, "where of course your worthy colleague will be, standing alongside me and my crew. I have no doubt he will be able to provide much guidance and ably represent the senate in this great enterprise."

Temorri looked pleased, a touch smug. "I am looking forward to launch Governor. As is my aide, Dawn."

Cassus suppressed a shudder. "It will be a pleasure to have you on board Senator."

Vil coughed. "So, when have you gentlemen planned for this ceremony to take place?"

"All in good time Vil. All in good time." Cassus declared.

*****

The ceremony took place a few days later in the senate voting hall, which was largely empty. Temorri and Lyron waited by a simple Actavian wooden table, a by-product of Cassus's *Dome Parks Programme*. On the table there a heavy tomb, an old-fashioned pen and a slim datapad. The table stood on a stage in the centre of the room which was surrounded on three sides by simple tiered voting benches. The senators were flanked by their aide de camps including the ponderous form of Dawn Haran.

Vil's partner Lilia sat on the first tier of voting benches in front of the table with their 8-year-old daughter Ivy, who waved. Vil's friend Alan Spartan, now a full Regulator in the Central Computer Department, sat next to Lilia and pulled funny faces at her. Stuart Bronzemerit, a journalist originally from Earth, sat a few rows above them speaking quietly into a datapad recorder. A small cluster of Regulators and Section Heads sat on the other side of the hall, heads close together in conversation.

Vil sat in an ante-chamber and fidgeted with his Star City section head sash as he waited to be called. His uniform was spotless, but slightly creased and a little tight around the waist. He could see part of the hall from a small window set into the wall. There was no sign of Cassus. He regretted having a second nutriboost and hoped that he wouldn't need to piss half way through the investiture ceremony.

*****

Senator Temorri beckoned for Vil to sit in the single chair on the nearside of the table as he and Lyron sat down on the other side. Vil was surprised when Lyron smiled at him and enquired, quite politely whether he was ready to proceed.

"Ready as I'll ever be. Where's the Governor though?"

Temorri raised his chin, indicating behind Vil. From out of a passage under the rear voting benches and directly connected to the Governor's suite, Cassus appeared. He strode purposefully, flanked by Brox and Colonel Hill, the commandant of the Acto security force. All wore full Actavian purple and black dress uniform, a black tunic with high collars and cuffs and knee high black synthetic boots. Cassus wore his Governor's heavy creamy white sash emblazoned with the blood red planetary symbol of Acto, its three cities, the Star City emblem and the spreading golden arrows of the Planetary Federation.

Cassus and Hill drew to an abrupt halt a few steps behind Vil who craned his head to see what was going on. Brox stood a pace behind them.

"Governor Cassus and Commander Hill" Brox thundered at parade ground volume, making the Senators jump. Vil grinned at them impudently.

Without waiting for prompting Cassus launched into his speech, "Senators Lyron and Temorri you have been *summoned* here today to witness this investiture. I, Cassus Toradon, Governor of Acto and the three cities do pronounce that of my own free will an executive order for the honourable position of Governor with all current terrestrial powers be transferred to Vil Toradon, currently Section Head of the Star City project, for a term of at least one year."

Vil stood and gave a half bow as Cassus stripped off his sash as he formally accepted the vestment in both hands.

Senators Lyron and Temorri authenticated the book in ink and with thumb print recognition on a triple encrypted solid state hard-drive and minutes later Vil Toradan had risen to the rank of Governor.

In his mind old ambitions flared unexpectedly and no longer smiling, Vil tugged on his uniform and cast a sombre gaze around the assembly. Cassus stepped back and bowed his head.

"Governor Vil Toradan!" came a shout from the benches and more voices joined the chorus.

'Governor indeed. All hail the Governor,' thought Vil as, in an instant, he was transformed from humble ex-tax inspector into the most powerful man on the planet and his heart thumped hard in his chest.

*****

Vil's Governorship would not technically commence until Cassus had left Acto's thin atmosphere and would not apply aboard the Perga where Cassus retained the title and powers invested in the role.

Over the next week the brothers worked side by side in their preparations for the grand celebrations to be held for the tenth anniversary since the old Administration was overthrown. The night's entertainment would culminate in the launch of the Perga and be broadcast not only on screens in every home and every public place on the planet Acto but eventually around the inhabited Galaxy.

On the evening before the planetary celebrations Cassus held a private party at the Governor's tower in Acto city-proper at the heart of the old colony dome. All ten of the Regulators from the central computer department would be in attendance as well as the hundred or so Section Heads who sat beneath them. Several senators were also invited including Senator Guy Royal, a staunch Toradan Administration supporter, Sejanus Lyron, Rosalind Corn and Grippus Temorri who would shortly be joining the crew of the Perga with his ever-present side kick Dawn Haran.

The Governor's accommodation, which had once seemed so palatial to a younger Cassus, now seemed slightly cramped; A utilitarian building hiding under a thin gloss of sophistication. The main audience hall and antechambers were all stuffed to bursting with Acto's elite, as they nibbled on fresh fruits from the city's hydro-domes.

From the raised stage a band from the Actavian

Academy played a selection of classics from the last five centuries.

A half smile touched Cassus's lips as he spied Alan Spartan, Vil's old school friend and now full Regulator of the hydroponics department. The two had grown close over the last decade as Cassus's ever growing responsibilities added more weight to his shoulders. Alan Spartan's light irreverence brought a sense of perspective to counter his growing power and influence.

Al was busy casting a professional eye over a small red and green apple before biting into it with something approaching glee.

"You'll keep an eye on him for me Alan?"

"Governor!" Alan spluttered, almost choking on a piece of apple. Overcome by a fit of coughing Alan tried to twist his arm around in a vain attempt to pat himself on the back. Cassus obligingly gave him a few solid thumps to aid his recovery.

"Hmmm, perhaps I should I ask Vil to keep an eye on you Al!"

"I've been assaulted by my own Governor, well there's one of my lifetime ambitions ticked off the old bucket list! I'm fine thank you Cassus. I think something went down the wrong way."

"Yes, I suspected that was the case Al."

"Don't you worry though chief. Me and the other regulators will keep an eye on Toradon junior." Al took a sly look around and in hushed tones added, "They are all on side you know, Lilia, Kathryn, Peterson, Milson and all the rest. Even old Dejean in Transportation."

Cassus nodded. "I do. It's the Senate I'm worried about."

"He'll manage Governor. The Toradons built this Administration. You have the support of the CCD's Regulators, Section Heads and the colonists."

"Yes, but so did my predecessor and look what happened to him!"

Al looked momentarily confounded and Cassus snorted in amusement. "Get back to the party Al and enjoy yourself. You deserve it. I'll see you in a few months."

"Take care of yourself Cassus. And that crew of yours. Vil will manage things here." Al waved goodbye as Cassus disappeared swiftly into the crowd shaking hands and offering a few words to his guests as he went. He didn't look back.

'Typical' thought Al. He looked a little forlorn until his fellow Regulator and Vil's partner, Lilia, joined him and put her arm through his.

"You'll see him again Al, I'm sure of it. The man's a natural born leader and a survivor." Lilia whispered into his ear.

"Oh, I know that. I'm more worried about your Toradan than that one. Where is he anyway?"

"He's meeting Cassus over at the Senate building in Novum City to say farewell. Then no doubt he'll be back here demanding a beer. Probably more than one."

Al looked fondly at Lilia "Well on that count at least I'm confident that we can help out our new Governor."

*****

Fireworks spread across the sky above the Domes and protective bubbles at high altitude and were met at ground level by fountains of bright lights bursting forth across each of Acto's three cities. Pushing back the darkness for a brief time in a cacophony of noise, a riot of colour. The new cafes and restaurants around the great senate square offered drinks and cuisines from across the inhabited Galaxy.

Holograms of Cassus, looking stern and resplendent were legion, posters hung from buildings across the planet, a few had even appeared of a modest looking Vil, who had secretly taken photographs of them for his album.

Cassus and Vil stood on the balcony overlooking the square.

"Very soon now Vil. My time here is drawing to a close."

"It's only a temporary arrangement Cassus."

"Do you think you'll find them?"

Cassus looked down, over the thrumming square below, his mouth set in a hard line.

"Hmmm. I don't know." Cassus thought for a few moments, brow creased.

"No, no I don't think so."

"There's always a chance. You're heading in the same direction."

"Yes, there's a chance," Cassus smiled over at Vil. "But don't be disappointed if I return without them. Space is a pretty big place you know." Cassus waved at the sky. "Ah, there they are. Look Vil, over there."

Vil turned his gaze towards the area his brother had indicated and after a second saw the faint glow of a precooled heat exchange engine in the distance. There were scores of them.

"There are so many," he gasped.

"It's almost the entire force." Cassus sounded satisfied.

The Actavian Space Force fly-by and display marked the pinnacle of the celebrations. All ten squadrons of twenty-four aircraft had been assembled in staggered formation. They flew low and slow, still above the Domes but clearly visible against the starlit sky. Acto's finest were joined by a squadron from Trestel, the droid specialist planet and closest neighbour of import. Under Cassus's administration trade and diplomatic relations had grown steadily closer. The ruling families of Trestel operated a limited form of democracy but their populace enjoyed incredible wealth thanks to their largely automated manufacturing industries and cutting-edge droid-tech.

The Actavian defence force had been thoroughly modernized over the last five years with the old Neotechnic class craft relegated to storage or sold off to the minor systems and local planetary transport defence. Cassus had even sent three to his old friend Coldor on his new rock of a home.

Acto's new *Cohort* class variant had been developed and manufactured indigenously with assistance from Trestel's R&D labs and was capable of spaceflight thanks to its Lynx Class engines which were in essence a much smaller version of the Panther Class engines used on the Perga.

"Time is ticking Cassus. You need to get to the crew."

"So eager to see me gone brother?"

"Ha! I'm still hoping you'll change your mind."

"It's too late for that. These could be our final moments together." Cassus said gravely.

Vil blinked. "No. I don't believe that. You'll be back. I don't want to do this for ever. Besides, if you delay too long, I'll have to redecorate the whole Senate building *and* Novum city just for good measure."

Cassus blew through his nose in amusement. "So be it. Keep the Senate under control for me Governor."

"That's affirmative Governor."

Cassus extended his hand and Vil clasped it firmly before sweeping Cassus into a brief embrace and thumping him several times on the back.

Governor Cassus gently disengaged himself and patted Vil on the shoulder again before walking back through the doors into the Senate house. He half turned before the doors glided closed and gave a small wave. Vil raised his hand in return but Cassus was already gone and he was left alone on the balcony to watch the afterglow bathe the sky in red.

*****

Cassus and Brox dumped the outbound EV in the parking lot outside Star City and waved to the waiting news crews without stopping. There were more than Cassus had expected. The pair made their way straight up to the lounge at the top of the Dome. Brox was uncharacteristically quiet.

"You ready Brox?" An invigorated Cassus asked.

"Yeah. This is really it then. Off into the deep."

"Into the deep my friend. There's still time if you want to change your mind you know."

"What!" Brox barked "and leave you to fend for yourself? I don't think so Governor. I volunteered for this and I'll see it through."

"Course you will. Come on, the crew are waiting and we're on a deadline."

Cassus and Brox stepped into the lounge and there for the first time saw the other three dozen or so members of the crew together in the same space. Cassus and Brox stood in the shadow of the entrance and after a few moments the crew ceased whatever they were doing and watched him expectantly. Cassus had prepared a few words in his head but in the heat of the moment these seemed contrived, even trite. Every man and woman assembled here knew what they were getting into, the months and in some cases years of training and preparation had all led up to this day, every second that ticked past had up led to this one moment in time, a spec in infinity and Cassus could not adequately express the enormity of it.

"Shall we?" he said and as a single body the crew followed their captain into the gloomy passage leading to the space elevator and beyond, up to the waiting bulk of the Perga.

CHAPTER 4

The crew spent the first two weeks acclimatizing to life on board the ship. The launch was broadcast across the inhabited galaxy as a bright streak of light high above the city domes of Acto. The wider Galaxy, well aware of this outbound journey had celebrated or grumbled according to their inclination. Some people thought the endeavour a colossal waste of money but many more took inspiration from it and perhaps some small measure of hope. Bronzemerit relayed a daily message from the Perga and stories from various members of the crew through the recently established Emprise News Station in Novum City. Bronzemerit's interest stories would be broadcast near continuously up until the first stasis phase in a month's time.

Cassus set a relaxed pace. He wanted the crew to adjust to their daily routines and get used to working the ship with each other outside of the training simulations back on Acto. The first port of call and first real test for the crew would be to dock with Acto's outermost celestial possession, a mining station positioned close to an asteroid belt rich in minerals. However, with the Panther engines running at quarter power it would take another week to reach the belt and Cassus and his officers wanted to get to know the ship and their crew better before taking the Perga out beyond the belt and into the unknown.

On the first day of the third week Cassus visited the droid storage hangar in the bowels of the vessel for the first time since his impromptu visit with Vil.

The hydraulic elevator hissed to a halt at the last stop at the end of the shaft and the doors pinged open. The ship's lights on this level were dim, similar to those last few minutes of dusk before the sun finally sets. The droid hangar lay at the far end of the corridor past several sealed storage bays on either side. Halfway down were steep flights of steps leading to the lowest levels of the ship and the launch hangars for the vertical drop landing craft, that were affectionately known as 'Pugs.' These squat little ships could also be launched from the main flight deck.

Cassus stepped out into the gloom and the overhead lights flicked on one after another. He stood and waited for a moment as his eyes adjusted and followed the trail of light to the droid hangar. The RDG class droids were still locked into their storage racks with the RDX droid immobile in front of the control console. Cassus reached round and pressed his thumb to a pad on the console which immediately lit up. Somewhat awkwardly he reached round t he droid and keyed in an old-fashioned security code. Withdrawing his arm Cassus stepped back and waited to see what would happen.

*****

Almost as soon as Cassus had powered up the RDX a glow seemed to emanate from deep within the torso of the droid and blossomed outwards across its body, limbs and extremities. Within a minute the droid raised its head and her eyes immediately fixing on Cassus.

"Hello Governor," she said.

Cassus had thought about whether to name the droid and had scanned several databases on naming protocols across systems that had embraced droid-tech to a greater degree than Acto but had instead opted for flicking through a data-pad of popular 20th century Western terrestrial names.

"So then Mandy, welcome to the crew." Cassus held out his hand.

The RDX looked down at the proffered hand and extended her own. Her grip was light and cool but not cold. Not unpleasant in fact. The droid's skin was not seamless, rather made up of thousands of tiny polymer panels perfectly aligned, hard but supple. It looked neither like human skin nor clothing but rather a form particular to the droid. Mandy was hairless but nonetheless far more humanoid in appearance than the practical RDG droids, which were advanced humanoid machines for sure but machines nonetheless. Mandy's form in contrast was disturbingly female with sweeping curves and a flared hip.

Cassus found he was gazing into Mandy's eyes. The most human element of her. One could almost believe they were human. They were the brightest blue of the summer sky and they gazed at him earnestly, never leaving his face.

"You don't mind being called Mandy? We don't have much experience with RDX class droids on Acto. I am not sure what the proprieties are." He released Mandy's hand.

Mandy's lips curled into a smile and she cocked her head. "I don't have much experience with humans Master Cassus but I look forward to learning. You can call me whatever you wish but Mandy will do just fine. I shall inform the others. Cassus followed her gaze to the hibernating RDG's.

"You can communicate with them in their standby mode?"

"No but I can install updates so that they are aware of any pertinent information when they are activated Master."

"Yes, of course." Cassus nodded once. "You don't need to call me Master. That is not my position to you. You will be a member of the crew. Captain will suffice for now. I'd like you to join us up on the bridge when you're ready to. You will be more use to me there than down here. I also want you operational when we go into hibernation next week."

"It will be as you command Captain."

Cassus cast his eyes over the droid. "Er, do you need a uniform?"

Mandy looked down at herself and cocked her head. "I am perfectly comfortable as I am Governor but can change my shell colour if you wish?" Without waiting for confirmation, the droid's shimmering silver colour dimmed and her body rapidly flooded with a flesh tone colour that spread out smoothly from her torso through to her limbs and breasts and finally inched along the fine features of her face and head. From more than a few inches away Mandy now appeared as a naked human woman; A startlingly attractive naked bald woman. Cassus's eyes widened as he took her in, suddenly conscious that if anyone were to see them it would appear as though he was standing with a naked woman tucked away in the bowels of the ship. Worse, he could feel himself reacting to her proximity. 'Shit, how long has it been,' he thought.

Pulling himself together under Mandy's unassuming eye, he managed "You'll be fine as you were Mandy. It's probably best not to change colour like that in front of the crew though. It would distract them. I didn't know you could even do that!"

Cassus could have sworn that a slight smirk appeared on Mandy's lips as her eyes flicked down to his trousers. "I understand Governor. Judging from your reaction, this ability may be startling to the crew. I can adopt any colour shell required, but will retain the colour I was created in, if that is your preference."

"Fine, fine," Cassus took a deep breath and blew out his cheeks. He left Mandy with the other droids in their chamber. As his sure footsteps echoed back down the corridor, he reflected that Mandy had said 'created'. He cast a look back to the chamber where Mandy stood immobile, silently watching him. She had returned to her usual silver casing as the lights switched off one by one behind him.

'Interesting choice of words' Cassus thought, tugging his uniform trousers back into place.

*****

"We are approaching the mining station Governor." Cassus was on the bridge with Brox and Sergeant Narcissa, FJ and Mandy. Ensign Sal Puar manned the comms stations and Lieutenant James Nosse monitored the Navigation displays whilst Chief Engineer Peter 'Bolt' Marcell hovered anxiously between the two of them. Stuart Bronzemerit watched eagerly with Senator Temorri from the tiny lounge area next to the refresh station.

"That's it?" Senator Temorri sounded disappointed.

"It's much smaller than I expected" Narcissa snorted and looked pointedly at Brox, who laughed.

"It's old," Chief Engineer Peter 'the Bolt' Marcell pointed out. "Been out here since before Governor Cole's time. The wealth of 'roid mining in this belt is one of the reasons Acto was established as a colony in the first place."

"Thanks for the history lesson professor," Narcissa yawned, to Bolt's annoyance.

"Do we dock with them or is it the other way round?" Bronzemerit mused out loud.

Bolt assumed the question was directed at him. "We'll be docking with them but we've got to take it nice and slow. I don't want to knock them out of alignment. I hope their computer is up to the task. Exa, have you established contact with the station mainframe?"

Exa's melodious tone filled the bridge, "the station's code and algorithms are antiquated but they are prepared for boarding."

"Don't get too comfortable. We're only here for a flying visit," Cassus said. He flicked a control on his uniform wrist pad and addressed the wider crew. "Attention all crew, this is the Captain speaking. We will shortly dock with mining station Deep Alpha 1. Assume your docking positions now. As you know, this is a brief stop-over. Only members of the command crew will be disembarking to pick up our final crew member. Cassus out."

"We're picking up a 'roid miner then chief? Brox asked.

"That's right. I want someone with on the ground experience as it were. Who better than an asteroid miner from Acto's furthest outpost?"

"Five minutes to docking Sir," Bolt stated.

Cassus looked around the assembled command crew, "To your seats please ladies and gentlemen."

"Don't forget Brox captain!" Narcissa sniggered. Brox beat his chest and grunted "Brox man too!" Narcissa laughed as he capered around a bemused looking FJ. "Pox! What the devil do you think you're doing?"

Cassus cocked his head, "Are we done? All right you two, if you've quite finished; seats please!"

The Perga whispered closer to the docking arm of the diminutive Alpha station. The behemoth dwarfed the old station and Cassus winced as the distance closed but Exa guided the ship in perfectly and reported a secure seal.

Cassus clapped his hands, "Let's go get ourselves a 'roid miner" and strode out of the bridge and towards the disembarkation airlocks.

*****

The heavy inner hatch to Alpha station opened in an audible strain of hydraulics and revealed a small cargo bay bedecked in floor to ceiling racks of various handheld equipment. There was nobody present to greet them, just the quiet hum of background machinery. Cassus frowned.

"Quite the reception they've prepared for us," said Narcissa who'd accompanied Cassus along with Senator Temorri, Brox, FJ, Bolt and Mandy.

Cassus peered around at the piles of equipment, "Connie is on her way."

"Connie?" Temorri probed.

Cassus nodded, "the Alpha Station chief. Chief mining engineer Connie Row."

Narcissa raised a long and sculpted eyebrow, "It's a woman then? In charge of this … Pile of junk."

Before Cassus could respond, the woman herself stepped through the hatch in the ante-chamber.

"Ah, I see," Narcissa murmured.

Connie Row was a formidable looking woman. She wasn't quite as tall as Narcissa being a shade under six foot, big boned but strong with it, her physique developed from wearing the heavy personal protective equipment used by miners on the asteroids. Like an ancient knight in armour, the weight of the full harness enhanced the wearers physical strength dramatically over time. Today though she was just wearing a sand-coloured one-piece suit tightly zipped up the front. Nylon patches with the emblem of Station Alpha were fixed to both shoulders with her name patch, slightly frayed, over her chest.

Cassus, who knew what to expect, thought that she was perhaps the strongest woman he would ever meet. Connie nodded to Cassus, who nodded back.

"Welcome to Alpha" she said.

"Hello Connie. We've arrived. I thought perhaps you were going to roll out the red carpet?"

"We don't have any red carpet Governor. Come to think of it we don't have any carpet". Connie stated straight-faced, although there might have been a twitch of an upturned lip.

"Here to pick up Boomer then? He's not in a good mood by the way. He'll miss the next 'roid tumble."

"Very possibly more than one Connie, but we'll find something to keep him occupied."

"Good. Best to keep him busy. Now I expect you'll be wanting a tour before you disembark?"

"Not this time Connie. Just here to pick up the package." Cassus gestured to Connie to proceed.

"What's a 'roid tumble?" Senator Temorri whispered to Chief Engineer Bolt.

"I expect it's a mining expedition of some sort," Bolt replied in hushed tones.

"Spot on. No need to whisper," Connie called back from over her shoulder as she led the party deeper in the station.

The corridor was wide and low, lit intermittently by low power diodes. They passed two intersections and a couple of curious station personnel dressed in the same sand-coloured suits. They didn't salute but Cassus nodded to them as they passed. In less than two minutes they reached a bank of three lifts. Connie walked straight to the central lift and barely paused as the doors pinged open.

"Turbo lift to station level 3," Connie requested.

After a rapid ascent the lift slowed and Connie shuffled to the front of the group and stepped out into an open domed chamber perhaps just over 100 foot in diameter, surrounded by heavily reinforced portholes and capped with an oculus at the crown of the dome. There were a dozen or so station crew lounging in booths, playing games or drinking at the central bar.

"Our rec centre" Connie announced. "Heart of the station really. Boomer will be in here if he's anywhere," she said to more herself than anyone else and scanned the room. "There he is, playing a holo game. Let's go grab you your 'roid miner Governor."

The off-duty occupants of the rec facility were all watching Cassus and crew as they traversed the room. A few threw waves, which Cassus dutifully returned.

Boomer was playing with two other miners, both physically big, physically powerful men crammed into a circular booth at one side of the room around a holo games table. Boomer was easily identifiable by his stature, with a barrel like chest and huge slabs of muscle around his upper body. Boomer's face was unshaven with tough looking, leathery pocked skin, fleshy cheeks and small but piercing bright blue eyes beneath a greasy mop of black hair showing a few greys. All three miners stood as Connie approached and nodded politely to Cassus but remained silent. Boomer pressed a small red button and the holo game froze on the table below them.

"Here they are then Boomer. You ready to ship out?"

"Aye chief. Dunnage stowed and ready to embark." Boomer's voice was as massive as the man. Starting deep in his belly amplified by his chest and forcibly ejected at volume from a square fleshy, unshaved face.

"You'll have to leave your game Boomer."

The older miner nodded. "To be expected. Will give these two time to practice whilst I'm gone. Well, so long boys. I'll finish spanking you when I get back. Watch the throttle on shuttle 2 – It's sticking." Boomer shook hands with his associates and turned to face Cassus.

"William I. Brock. Your nickname is well earned. Are you prepared to join my crew aboard the Perga?"

"Reporting for duty, as ordered. Governor."

Boomer shot a glance over and up at Brox who stood close to Cassus's shoulder like a second shadow. Brox loomed over Boomer in height but despite his size was smaller in the chest and shoulders. The two men sized each other up in an instant.

"I will need you to inspect the landing equipment immediately upon embarking," Cassus continued.

Boomer returned his gaze to the Governor. "If it's not up to spec you'll be the first to know."

Cassus nodded. "Let us be about it then," turned on his heel and strode away purposefully, almost marching. The senior officers were swept up behind him. Boomer shrugged, sharing a long look with Connie.

"I'll be back eventually chief. Don't let the station fall apart without me."

"Ha! You not being here will give me the time I need to put it back together again!" Despite the playful words between two long serving friends, Brox noticed that

Connie took Boomer's hand in both of hers and squeezed it firmly before letting him go. Boomer's face moved in what could have almost passed for a grin.

The walk back to the cargo back was quick and quiet. Cassus gestured for the others to follow Brox back on to the ship and ducked back into the station to have a final word with Connie.

*****

Later the next day Cassus and Mandy met with Boomer in the second cargo bay on level eleven, the lowest deck of the ship. Two levels below the double flight deck where the Perga's four Cohort class fighters and transport craft were stored. The entire bay was stuffed with closely packed heavy ground equipment lined up in neat rows behind a wide central passage with four wide ramps down to the loading hangers for the Perga's Pugs or other craft. The lifts terminated at the other end of the cargo bay.

Cassus and Mandy walked up the central passage and looked around. Amongst the neat rows there were bulky mining and construction machines on tough looking industrial grade half-tracks. Several sleek looking rovers, called *Ferrets,* sat next to them. These had a six-wheel drive system, each wheel standing over five feet in height. There were also lighter wheeled scouting and exploration OEV's based on the same design as the OEV Cassus and Brox had recently driven to Star City. At the far end of the cargo area there were two rugged looking attack pods; A modern version of the vehicle that Vil had taken into battle again Governor Sendrick's forces a decade ago.

Exactly half way between the ramps were two mechanic stations with an automated circular turntable to move any of the machines around 360 degrees and powerful hydraulics to lift them along with various pulleys and manoeuvrable cranes. Cassus and Mandy found Boomer deep in conversation with two of crew's three dedicated ground crew mechanics, Jez Lloyd and Wyles. A half-disassembled rover was partially elevated on the turntable.

"Good afternoon Gentleman!" Cassus called.

"Good afternoon Captain" all three responded. The mechanics perhaps more vigorously than Boomer.

"How are you getting on boys?"

"All good Captain." Jez declared chirpily.

"Is there anything I need to know about? We'll be using some of this equipment at our next stopover. Boomer, I'd like your opinion."

Boomer glanced around the cargo bay, "I can't complain about any of the hardwear. It's precision made with quality materials, as it should be seeing as I chose half of 'em. The real test will be the people. When do we eventually get round to using some of this stuff?"

"That's why you're here Boomer. We need your expertise to train the crew, get them comfortable with using the machines."

"How much time will I have?"

Cassus gave a half smile, "long enough."

"I'll see you all at the briefing in a month, once we come out of stasis!"

*****

"Are the crew all prepped for the first round of stasis Doc," Cassus asked his chief medical officer.

"Ready as they'll ever be Captain. Brox is still grumbling about it and I'd like to monitor FJ myself for the first stasis period given his advancing years, but the crew are in good shape" Doctor Catlea informed him.

The Doctor was in her early 40's, just shy of 5'5" and well-toned with dusky skin and long ebony hair that alternated between being straight and frizzy seemingly at random. She has been the Toradon's doctor for almost 10 years and had volunteered for duty aboard the Perga as soon as she'd learned about the mission. Catlea also had a young family back on Acto and only with a great deal of reluctance had Cassus accepted her application to join the crew.

"The first jump will be the shortest. I want to bring us down to hypersonic flight and bring the crew back to operating efficiency as soon as it's safe to do so," Cassus explained.

Catlea thought for a moment or two, "There is no reason why we cannot have the crew returned to normal duties within a couple of days after coming out of stasis. Light duties only for the first 24 hours would be my recommendation."

"Very good doc. The first crew members will be reporting to you within the hour. We'll run a full rotation with my turn in a week's time."

"Are you able to let me know our next destination? Anything I need to prepare for?"

"I will and there will be. I'm planning on testing out some of our heavy ground equipment. I won't give you the details because I want to see how the crew copes with a real training exercise outside of the simulations. Expect some bruises Doc! I'll see you in a few days so you can put me under."

CHAPTER 5

Cassus and Mandy were in the observation floor of the hibernation chamber. Most of the crew were now in stage one hibernation and securely strapped into their capsules, which were almost entirely transparent and allowed 360-degree visibility of the occupants.

As Cassus inspected the readings on each pod he noted with some amusement that everyone was wearing regulation pants with the exception of Sergeant Narcissa who was wearing a camo pattern thong and the journalist Stuart Bronzemerit who was wearing what appeared to be some sort of tiger print briefs.

Mandy stopped in front of Brox and raised the ridges that passed for her eyebrows. "The readings are one hundred per cent but, he doesn't look entirely comfortable Governor."

Cassus finished checking Bolt Marcell's pod and joined Mandy. "Oh, don't worry Mandy; That's his natural expression. He's disliked the hibernation process from day one. Says the tubes irritate his throat."

Mandy examined Brox for a moment more. "He has extremely well-developed musculature. I estimate virtually 200 pounds."

Cassus glanced at the data stream which read 199.6 pounds. "You're spot on Mandy. He's a fine example of a man."

Mandy switched her skin colour so swiftly that Cassus almost missed the change. She now matched Brox's darker skin tones exactly. Before Cassus could react, she switched back to her metallic norm.

"You're getting better at that Mandy" Cassus said, bemused.

"It was quicker to match the pigment this time," the droid confirmed. "I trust you are not dissatisfied. As none of the crew are currently operational on this level, I have not disobeyed your instructions."

Cassus grunted, "That's fine but next time some warning please."

"As you instruct Governor." Mandy was quiet for moment and then turned back to face Cassus. "He is your friend." She pointed at Brox.

Cassus nodded, waiting to see what the droid would say next.

"I find the concept intriguing. I would like to learn more about friendship. Especially from you."

"Why me?"

The droid thought for a moment. "You hold a position of immense power, at least on your own planet and certainly aboard this ship and yet I have observed that you seem to have many friends here amongst the crew."

"I do my best."

"I have yet to witness first-hand extended human interactions but I surmise that some people might be tempted to take advantage of your nature to further their own ambitions. I will watch this for you Governor and report to you should you so wish."

Cassus was about to decline, he didn't need a robotic snoop on his ship and besides he knew more than half the people aboard for at least several years. 'But what about the rest,' a small voice in his mind said. He bit his lip in thought and indicated that Mandy should sit on a row of flight chairs on the observation deck. He watched her as she gracefully folded herself into a chair and crossed her legs. Cassus contemplated whether that was her natural angle of repose, programming or observational learning from some of the women on the crew. He'd caught her observing Sergeant Narcissa's easy grace more than once. He sat down next to her and she watched him languidly.

Cassus leaned in, "Spying on one's crew is not an honourable course of action Mandy. It is not how Governor's or indeed righteous men should behave. Nonetheless, my honour may not be the most important factor here and I am not a wholly righteous man." Cassus tapped his chair arm firmly with a fingernail, "The mission must survive and nothing must be allowed to jeopardise it."

"Why is this mission so important to you Governor?"

"It is not the mission. I fully expect the mission to fail. It is the act that counts. Mankind must be galvanized to keep satisfying our innate curiosity, our quest for ever increasing knowledge to dispel the malingering miasma of stone-age superstitions, blind faith, fanatical dogma and the rise of ignorance and destructive revisionism. Science and progress must be the answer to our stagnation. This outbound voyage is being watched by the countless millions across the colonised galaxy. It is the first in a generation and must not be the last in my time. The attempt is everything."

"What of the crew?"

Cassus started to tap his chair again. "If I bring them home safe and others see that, then I will have achieved enough for people to take notice. Don't forget, they are all here because they want to be part of this journey. Most of them anyway."

Mandy pondered for a minute. "There is much to assess here. Thank you for the instruction Governor."

Cassus realised with a jolt that the droid had copied him and leaned towards him. Her face was mere inches from his own. For a moment he wondered what it would be like to kiss that beautiful but cold visage and whether such a thing was in fact possible. Intrigued and perhaps slightly revolted Cassus quickly retreated to complete his tour of the capsules, leaving the RDX series droid to watch him quietly once again.

*****

The transparent foam of the hibernation pod moulded itself to fit the contours of Cassus's body. It was firm but yielding. Doctor Catlea strapped him in and prepared the stasis tubes and equipment as Commander Elara and Mandy looked on.

"You're all set Captain. As soon as you're ready we can begin the hibernation process and we'll see you again in a month."

Cassus turned his head slightly towards Elara, "You'll be in command El. As soon as I go under. It will just be you, Lieutenant Nosse, the Doc and a couple of the Ops crew and Boomer. Oh, and Mandy of course." Cassus winked at Elara, "I expect the ship to still have all its constituent parts when I wake up!"

"But Captain, I was going to jettison all non-essential personnel as soon as you're asleep. Starting with those tin cans you keep locked up on the lower decks …" Elara replied as Doctor Catlea manipulated some controls on a panel to one side of the hibernation capsule and close to Cassus's head.

Cassus smiled and closed his eyes.

Doctor Catlea leant over the prone form of the Captain and felt his pulse, "He's asleep," she advised softly and the two women and a feminine droid left the stasis chamber silently, despite there being no possibility of anyone coming out of stasis naturally. The transparent protective shell of the capsule glided into place and latched firmly shut with a faint hiss.

*****

Vil sat behind his new desk in the Senate and spun his chair round at an alarming speed, whistling to himself.

Eventually the chair slowed to a stop and he rocked backward and forwards for a few moments.

"Well, this is a complete waste of time" he muttered and hit a button on his desk that activated a pop-up screen with various items of information and data feeds from the CCD and other sources. He gave the data little more than a cursory glance and nothing piqued his interest. Senator Lyron was already ten minutes late to their weekly meeting. Vil's mood was fatuous and deteriorating quickly. He chewed his lip, the Senator wouldn't have dared to turn up this late when Cassus was Governor and where the hell was Senator Royal, his principle political adviser.

"Duster!" Vil called to the guard on duty inside the door, "Can you poke your head out and see whether Senator Lyron is deigning to visit us this morning?"

Roland Sleeth was in his early twenties and unusually for the Actavian Guard was growing a moustache, which he spent considerable time nurturing, earning him the nickname Duster from his colleagues and new boss.

Duster scanned the corridor for a few seconds and popped his back into Vil's office, "He's right here Sir. Must have just arrived," he reported.

"Senator Lyron, Sir!" Duster announced unnecessarily.

Vil raised an eyebrow, "Well, show him in then Duster."

"Sir!"

The Senator slipped into the room as smooth as silk, "Good morning Governor, I trust this day finds you well?"

Vil glanced at the clock on his screen, "It *is* still morning Senator, but we're rapidly running out of it. Where have you been?"

"My apologies Governor, I was detained by the arrival of a report from the outer Novum patrol. I thought you'd want to see it immediately." The Senator held out a flat chip half the size of a thumb and nodded.

"A physical copy Senator?"

"You'll want to keep this on an eyes-only basis for cleared personnel."

"You've read the report?"

"I have and then I brought it straight here to you. I'd advise you to read it Governor".

Vil eyed the Senator for a moment, took the chip and slotted it into a bank of ports on his desk. The file name appeared on the pop-up screen and Vil started an audio command to open it. Nothing he happened. He stopped, tilted his head, considering, "Audio command disabled Lyron?"

There was a hint of a smile on the Senators face. He nodded again. "Password as follows - NOVDSAM3." Vil double tapped the file name and slid open a compartment on his desktop. A standard touch keyboard popped up and Vil typed in the password himself.

A routine report template from the Actavian Security Force mobile division popped up with entries for date, time, location, personnel and weather. Below these fields was a box for additional comments by the patrol commander.

"The reports are made vocally. Their personal computer transcribes the words to the written report automatically," Lyron supplied helpfully.

The commander in this case, Sergeant Baker, had logged a series of routine entries as he'd completed a sweep around the perimeter of Novum city and then commenced a wider sweep. Baker then noted glimpsing something flashing under the bright sun and had made the decision to alter course and investigate.

The next comment was entered half an hour later. Baker and his crewmate had spotted something half buried under the shifting sands close to a great outcrop of black granite. Upon closer inspection they'd pulled an antenna from the dunes, stating that it looked like an OEV communications antenna. They'd moved to inspect the nearby rocks and uncovered the buggy itself, almost buried in the sands but unoccupied.

Vil's eyes sped over the words, a kind of sick excitement budding within him.

The next entry to the report was time dated ten minutes later. The security force had found the edge of a patch of sand blasted into glass and after digging part of it out had concluded that a small one or two man ship had launched from that spot several years ago.

"It can only be one person Governor."

Vil's gaze moved slowly towards the Senator.

"And who do you propose that might that be Lyron?"

The Senator looked surprised; the emotion slicked across his face like oil across still water. "Why, Governor Sendrick of course. He may still be alive. He may still be out there!" and the Senator gestured grandly towards the stars.

Vil looked blank but his mind was whirling and his fingers drummed against his desk, tap, tap.

Tap, tap, tap.

*****

"Welcome back Captain"

Cassus opened his eyes and found himself looking into the kindly eyes of Doctor Catlea. Momentarily bewildered, he cast around and then, in an instant, reality came flooding back and he met the Doctor's eye and smiled. Elara and Brox were standing behind the Doctor. Brox towering over her and Elara peeking over her shoulder.

Cassus waved at them all and said, "Good to be back Doc."

"Elara, have we reached the system?"

"Yes Captain, we entered the target system at 0400 hours this morning."

"Excellent!" cried Cassus. "And the crew?"

"There's a few still need defrosting but the whole crew will be available for the briefing at 1800."

"Brox, how was the hibernation for you? I feel a little groggy."

Brox reflected for a second, "There weren't any pan pipes so I think I can live with it Captain."

Cassus laughed and motioned for Brox to help him out of the pod.

"Easy there Cassus," Doctor Catlea remonstrated, "it will take a little while for the effects of the hibernation to wear off; especially as this was your first time."

Cassis, supported by Brox, took a step over to Catlea and patted her on the shoulder fondly, "I'll be fine Doc."

"Do you fancy a coffee Captain?" Brox asked.

"You are my way of thinking entirely! C'mon Brox, let's get to the nearest refresh station."

The next few hours ticked past and under doctor's orders, Cassus took his leisure. Truth be told he didn't feel ready for much more than sipping hot coffee and munching the occasional snack. He worked in his ready-room adjacent to his cabin on level three, reviewing his notes for the pending briefing at the small conference table that ran the length of most of the room.

"Exa, what time is it?"

The time is 1702 hours" The ship's computer informed him. The ship's night and day cycle had been set to exactly match the rotation of Acto around its yellow Dwarf star, Darado Minor.

'Just under an hour remaining,' mused Cassus. He flipped his data pad closed and walked over to his cabin to check his appearance in the full height mirror, it wouldn't do to appear shabby in front of the entire crew.

"You have a guest waiting captain," announced Exa.

"Hmmm, I wasn't expecting anyone." Cassus said quietly to himself. "Come," he called walking back to the ready room.

The door slid open and Elara stepped through. "Hello Captain" she said.

"Elara! I was just getting ready for the briefing. I thought we were meeting in the conference room?"

"Aye, but I wanted to see you first and see how you are after stasis. Welfare falls within my purview under safety officer you know!"

Cassus gestured for Elara to take one of the comfortable chairs dotted around the conference table. He took the next seat to her. "No need to be concerned El. I'm fine. Bit woozy but functioning." Cassus pressed Elara's forearm briefly. A gentle pressure.

"You sound like that droid of yours!" she responded, glancing down,

"Hah! I don't think Mandy know the word 'woozy'. We're coming up to our first test as a crew. Do you think they're ready?"

Elara considered her words carefully, "We have the technology of course and the technical expertise. There's a lot of unknowns but we also need to learn to bond and work together as a crew."

"My thinking entirely. Come on, it'll be fine. Let's get over to the briefing room and grab a coffee. I want to be there as the crew arrive. It will be first time since we embarked that we're all together in the same room.

The ship's main briefing room was on the second deck behind a sealable bulkhead, a short walk from the officers' cabins. It occupied the wide sweep of the nose of the Perga and sat immediately above an identically sized room that provided the ship's main bar and recreation space and was a popular spot for off duty Pergans to relax and enjoy a game or a beer. It was as yet unnamed, simply being referred to as 3Bar. The briefing room above had already been given the moniker of 2brief or 'be brief' which amused the more juvenile members of the crew.

Cassus and Elara arrived first and stationed themselves

on a small raised plinth to one side of the space, which could accommodate twice the number of people currently aboard the ship.

The crew started to arrive in dribs and drabs. Cassus watched keenly as even with less than forty people onboard, several core groups had already started to emerge below the bridge crew. The flight crew rolled in, waved to the mechanics who were standing with the ground crew. The science bods rambled in, deep in conversation and moved to sit near the front alongside Professor Eston Cousteau, the Perga's expert in planetary archaeology. Eston was reading. Reading an actual book. Elara nudged Cassus gently in the ribs and nodded at him discretely, raising one eyebrow. He smiled as the final members of the Perga's small crew arrived and settled down. He noted Mandy at the back by the bar and waved at the silent droid, who waved back.

"Pergans!" Cassus announced, "Welcome! Everyone comfortable? FJ, you got your nutriboost? Yes? Good! Then let us begin!"

*****

Vil paced around his new apartment in Novum city, agitated. He paused by his desk to look at a three-dimensional holo-pic of himself and Lilia, Cassus and Octavia, Colder and their friend Alan Spartan grinning and hugging each other. The shot had been taken a year after the Toradon's had risen to power. Cassus was still seeing Octavia and looked flushed with excitement and pride. They were standing in front of the on the steps up the recently completed and refurbished Senate House. Even Coldor's normally stern visage had broken into a smile. Perhaps influenced by the bottles of synth-prosecco they were all waving around. Vil reached out to touch the image, his hand hovering on the edge of the display.

"Why so forlorn darling?" Lilia had been watching Vil from the comfort of an oversized chair on the other side of the snug room, which was decorating with momentos and huge landscape photos and even paintings of Acto's untamed, wild and dangerous landscape. Still largely untouched despite the development born under Governor Sendrick and accelerated under the Toradons.

"Sorry Lil. It's the news from yesterday. I hadn't thought about the Governor for years."

"You mean Governor Sendrick?"

Vil nodded, "Yes, the old Governor. When the searches stopped and we hadn't found him I thought that was it. It was over."

"You didn't have the same resources back in those days Vil. It was ten years ago. We all thought he'd gone."

"That's just it isn't it, where has he gone? Doesn't look like he died here and the evidence was right under our noses all this time."

"What are you going to do?"

Vil's gaze swept over to Lilia, still trim, still incredibly beautiful, her deep green eyes watching him with concern. Vil thought for the millionth time how lucky he was.

"I don't know yet. I'll send a space burst message to Cassus on the Perga tomorrow but other than that I could do with some advice."

"Shall we go out then? See if we can get some of the old gang together?"

Vil smiled for the first time that evening. "How about Palasantos?"

*****

"We are about to embark on the first real test of our mission!" Cassus cried. His excitement, for once, bubbling out as he leaned in towards the crew, speaking faster than normal.

"In less than two days we will begin our first real test together as a crew. After our first stasis period I am pleased to announced that the Perga has entered a planetary system in the early hours of this morning - Acto time."

There were some nods and shared looks of satisfaction from amongst the crew.

"This is star system K2 – 450b, a red dwarf star system. Stuart will be running a competition over the coming week to choose a more appropriate name..." Cassus paused, "Once we've landed there!"

Acto's favourite journalist, Stuart Bronzemerit gave a cheery wave and thumbs up around the crowd. "Get your thinking caps on people. Only sensible suggestions will be considered for this competition. That means no profanities and no references to phalluses or your genitals in general. No matter how special you may think they are."

A ripple of laughter preceded a sudden buzz of chat that swept through the room as Cassus pressed on, gesturing genially for some quiet, "There are only four planets in the system and none in the habitable zone. We have already passed two of these. The remaining planets are both super-terran gas planets. We have detected several moons in the system and are now on a heading towards the largest moon orbiting the closest planet. For the sake of having something to call it I have taken the liberty of naming the planet as 'Perga's Dawn' and this particular moon as 'Perga Minor'. We should be in orbit by late tonight or early tomorrow morning." Cassus looked at the Perga's navigator enquiringly, James Nosse, who nodded soberly back.

Your section leaders will brief you all in more detail before the days final watch and notify you who will be joining each landing crew. Mandy will pilot a lander in the second wave to begin testing our first complement of droids." Cassus glanced over at the RDX droid who hadn't appeared to have moved an inch since Cassus began his address.

"Every member of the crew will be expected to make at least one landing during our stay here." Cassus shifted his body and addressed the Senator and his aide, "Senator Temorri and Ms Haran as members of the crew, that order will of course include you. Your section leader is Commander Elara Blanc," Cassus rested two fingers on Elara's nearby shoulder, "so you'll be in good hands. The first wave will disembark at 0600. I will command. Now, I'm sure you have some questions!"

*****

Before the crew had dispersed Cassus had suggested that they dine together early in the evening before the first landings on the moon. The crew had, as a body, taken this to be an order and arrived en masse in the main dining hall on level four. The nutrition for the crew was largely automated and directed by the ship's nutritionist, Isabelle Grey who was known as Izzy. Unofficially, the Perga enjoyed the company of a human chef in the shapely form of Corporal Charlotte Chet. The Corporal was a member of the Ground Ops unit under Sergeant Lowery. Charlotte, or Triple C, as she had been immediately nicknamed was a competent NCO but a genius in the kitchen. Her 'home cooking' in great demand from the rest of the crew. She was normally assisted by Izzy and the mechanic Wyles, who had no real culinary skill beyond absurdly efficient and precise chopping, but was shamelessly interested in sampling more than Charlotte's proffered gustatory delights.

The thirty plus crew members piled into mountains of paella and nutriboosts or beer depending on their inclination. Cassus, now informal and relaxed, swigged from a ship issue beer and circulated slowly amongst the benches containing his crew, closely shadowed by Elara and Mandy. He clapped backs, shook hands and exchanged small-talk. He paused behind Boomer, still unsure of their relationship; half minded for a moment to press on but duty reared its head again and he paused. Brox who was sitting opposite the miner and next to Narcissa raised his eyebrows, not particularly subtlety, and pointed with his eyes. Cassus pretended not to notice. Brox said, "evening Captain. Big day tomorrow!"

Cassus grinned "Our first real test Brox. You're not flying one of the landers are you? I'd kind of hoped to make it down there with all my teeth still in my mouth."

Narcissa sniggered and even Boomer cracked a half smile. Brox, lubricated by a couple of beverages smiled easily "Not on the way down Sir. The Flight Lieutenant has got me on return duty for the second flight back though!"

"Well, that's wonderful Brox. Just try not to miss the target ok? It's a bit smaller than the moon." Cassus leant forward slightly towards Boomer "I'll see you on the surface. Don't stay up too late all." He raised a hand to clap Boomer on the back but hesitated. Instead he gave a rather awkward little wave and quickly turned away but was pleased to hear a chorus of "Aye Sir" from Brox, Narcissa and Boomer.

"I saved you a seat Captain!" Elara waved from her bench. She was sitting near the end of the hall, opposite FJ and his science officer, Doctor Lisa Tyne, who were already tucking into their paella.

"Good evening!" Cassus greeted them as he took his seat.

"Hello dear boy! I must say this food is quite remarkable!" FJ remarked, shovelling another parcel into his mouth.

"Do you not chew FJ?" Elara quipped as the older man devoured his meal with great enthusiasm. Lisa Tyne smiled at him fondly and said "Not so quickly FJ. You'll give yourself indigestion – Again!"

Elara beckoned to the kitchen crew and pointed at Cassus. Triple C acknowledged and spooned a great helping onto a ship issue recyclable plate for the Captain.

Charlotte Chet brought Cassus his helping herself, "Here you go Captain. Freshly made this afternoon."

"Thank you, Charlotte!" Cassus said, taking a mouthful and smiling in genuine pleasure, "Delicious! You're wasted in Ground Ops. Perhaps I should assign you to the position of ship's chef on a more permanent basis..."

FJ paused and eyed Cassus and Charlotte, a serious look upon his face, "May I just say that in all seriousness I believe that to be splendid idea!"

"Lovely thought FJ, but you'd get fat!" Lisa said playfully.

The older scientist nodded thoughtfully. "You're probably right my dear."

"Which flight are you assigned to Charlotte?" Cassus asked

"I'm on the second, seventh and penultimate flight down Sir, with Sergeant Lowery."

"You're in good hands then Charlotte, or should I say Triple C. Thank you for taking the time out to cook for us this evening and please thank Izzy and Wyles for me."

"I will Sir. It's a real pleasure Captain. I'd better get back though, before Wyles boils something he shouldn't!"

Cassus nodded at her and dived into his own dinner surrounded by the informal chatter of his crew as he thought hard about what the dawn would bring in this new system; an untouched satellite of a virgin world.

CHAPTER 6

Cassus's landing crew had assembled at 0530 on deck nine – The main flight deck at the rear of the ship. As well as the four cohort class fighters the Perga also possessed eight landing craft that resembled fat, squat shuttles with massive heat shields and quadruple extended rear fins. Half these vessels were nestled into the vertical drop hangers on deck eleven, the remainder stood on the flight deck. Their manufacturers name had quicky been replaced by 'The Pug'. The Pugs had a single pilot cabin and could ferry 6 suited passengers and some cargo or more if the passengers relied on the ship's own limited life support system. Alternatively, the ship could be easily reconfigured through demountable bulkheads to carry more cargo and less personnel.

The pilot of the second landing ship was Ensign Kel Fox, only recently graduated from Acto's burgeoning Academy. Kel was short and blond with a noticeably feminine figure under her plain jumpsuit uniform. She had volunteered for the mission before she was out of the Academy and Cassus knew her passably well from shared training simulations back on Acto. She was all business this morning though as Cassus attempted to stifle a yawn.

"Captain! Lander two is prepped and ready to disembark at your order, Sir!"

"Very good Ensign!" Cassus responded, straightening slightly. The rest of his crew were just performing their suit checks with variable degrees of competence. The crew considered of Sergeant Narcissa, Wyles the mechanic, FJ, Professor Eston Cousteau and Mandy. An exasperated Sergeant Narcissa was carefully double-checking FJ and Eston's suit prep for the second time. "Stay still man!" she was instructing as the archaeologist gesticulated at the marvels of the flight deck. FJ, never afraid of some exaggerated arm movements himself, enthusiastically joined in as the two oldest men on the ship continued their conversation, paying less attention to suit safety than was perhaps desirable.

"They're like school boys going on an outbound trip!"

Eston spun around, arms flailing as he pointed out some spare stacked Cohort wing sections to FJ. Narcissa, who was pressed close to his back checking his various suit feeds, had to swivel adroitly on her hip and duck to avoid being hit. The two ended in an awkward looking half embrace, with Eston, still talking to FJ, absently patting her on the back with his only free arm.

Cassus shook his head slightly. Was it his imagination of was the normally imperturbable Sergeant's dark skin looking flushed? "You're surprisingly strong for an old codg... I mean er, older gentleman" Narcissa remarked, as she managed to extract herself gently but firmly and then steered both men towards the lander by way of a firm hand on each of their backs. They sauntered up the ramp quite happily.

"Did you have to put *both* of them in your group boss?" She protested as she passed Cassus, who merely nodded, straight-faced.

"Let's get this show underway then." Cassus clapped cheerfully as Narcissa and her charges disappeared into the lander.

Cassus lent down and said quietly to Ensign Fox, "It's over to you now Ensign. Get us safely to the surface. I know you won't let us down."

"Aye Sir!" Ensign Kel Fox saluted. From across the deck her superior officer, Lieutenant Scholes, a plain-spoken man from Acto's smallest and most northerly city, waved encouragingly before climbing into his own ship. Ensign Fox gulped, took a deep breath and followed her captain into the landing craft, past her passengers who were in various states of preparation and climbed up into the familiar space of her small cabin.

*****

Vil tucked into his potato bravas and pan tumaca with gusto, surprised at his sudden appetite. The potatoes were even potatoes Alan Spartan announced proudly after inspecting them closely.

Lilia had managed to assemble a surprising number of people at such short notice. As well as Alan Spartan, a co-conspirator from before the rising against Governor Sendrick's Administration, they were joined by Lucinda Grey who had shared time with Vil as a conscript, Regulator Greggory Milson from Atmospheric control and his partner and Senator Guy Royal. Vil's dutiful young guard, Duster, had also insisted on coming and Vil had in turn insisted that he join them for something to eat. The Senator had also brought a security detail but they had not been invited to join the party and patrolled more or less vigilantly outside. The illustrious company has been ushered respectfully to the best table in the house. This stood on its own on a raised stage area near the front of the main dining room which overlooked a corner of the monumental square that could be glimpsed through lush foliage around the alfresco dining area.

Vil had already guzzled a couple of the restaurants own craft beers and tongue duly loosened, proceeded to inform his dinner guests of the latest news. Vil and Lilia quickly filled them in with the details and answered the inevitable questions as best they could.

"Cast aside your doubts folks, the data is reliable. It's real. Unfortunately for us."

"What are you going to do now Vil? Lyron won't sit still on this you know," Senator Royal advised.

"I was rather hoping to get some ideas off you lot! I'll let Cassus know of course. In fact, I sent a space-burst message to the Perga earlier today but it won't reach him for at least a week. Maybe more for all I know."

"Have they been through a stasis cycle now?" Regulator Milson asked.

"Yes, the first stasis cycle should have completed." Lilia filled in as Vil munched a croquette.

"I'm not sure there's anything Cassus can do," Vil pointed out crunchily, his mouth half full. "He's not going to turn the ship around. This is too important to him. Us."

"I'm afraid you're right Governor. I can't see him coming back until he's ready to." Milson commented.

"Maybe not even then," Vil grunted. "No. No, this one is on me. I will need to deal with Lyron and his pack of cronies."

"He has powerful friends in the Senate Vil" Lilia warned.

Vil swigged his Palasontos ale and gave a single exaggerated nod. A very Cassus style nod Lilia thought to herself.

"True, but on this planet, no-one is as powerful as the Toradons. He needs to remember that."

There was agreement around the table although Milson and Royal continued to look grave.

"I will call a meeting at the Senate for tomorrow – I want all our strongest supporters in attendance. Including Commander Perterson from the Guard."

"Is the Senate a wise choice Vil?" Guy Royal mused his forehead creased.

"We've nothing to hide Guy. Lyron and his cronies are well informed. They'd find out soon enough anyway and I'm not hiding from that little … shit stain. We'll meet at the Senate in plain view and put this on the table. Fair and square."

Duster meanwhile had ignored the conversation and instead concentrated on devouring on a large bowl of chorizo.

"Duster!" Vil cried.

Duster jumped and paused with a loaded fork half way to his mouth, "Governor?"

"Can you save me some tiny morsel from that delicious looking dish please."

"What is this made of anyway?" Alan asked. Spearing a slither on his fork and inspecting it. "Surely, it can't be actual pork, can it?"

Duster looked puzzled, "Pork? What is pork?" he asked.

*****

Kel Fox gripped her controls tightly, suddenly she was too hot in her uniform and the cabin which she'd always thought of as cosy, seemed too cramped. "Relax Kel. Get a grip of yourself" she admonished herself. The young Ensign took a deep breath and breathed out through her nose. She repeated this several times, focusing on just breathing. Tongue between her teeth she started the pre-flight sequence and looked left over to Lieutenant Scholes' ship which was waiting for Zarnes Man, one of the ground crew, to complete her external safety checks. Zarnes completed her routine and gave the thumbs up to Scholes who returned the gesture and waited for the remaining ground crew to move to a safe distance. The fat little shuttle trundled forward on its narrow ramp past the pressurized zone of the hanger and into the launch bay. Zarnes spoke into her control pad and nodded up at the little two-man control room that sat like a limpet on top of a narrow movable gantry that reached the ceiling of the hanger.

Second Engineer Jemmy Chadrick was in command of all the day's launches. He responded to Zarnes and began the sequence to open the triple hanger doors that slid silently open to unveil the cold desolation of space.

Kel watched Scholes craft power up and, as soon as the hanger doors were completely open, shot out into space, its engines flaring as the power engaged. "By the book as ever" Kel smiled to herself and looked out of her cockpit to see Zarnes on the deck checking her own lander. The second launch of the day. She knew she wouldn't get clearance until Scholes had cleared the moon's thin atmosphere but the seconds were ticking away at four times their normal speed.

Kel gulped as Zarnes completed her checks and gave her the thumb up. She waited until Kel had acknowledged her, spoke to control and then jogged back towards the first launch bay where the next lander was waiting.

Kel's headset buzzed into life. "Ensign Fox this is control you are cleared for launch. All systems are green. Please acknowledge."

"Hi Jemmy. Acknowledged and … ready for launch."

"You alright Kel? It's just another launch. You've done this a hundred times and have a hundred hours of test flights under your belt. It's no different this time. Just another day."

Kel Fox raised an eyebrow "Easy for you to say and it's one hundred and ten hours actually," she said to herself and her wiped her hands on her thighs as the lander began is short journey along the ramp to the depressurized zone and the waiting moon of Perga Minor that sat quietly in the void waiting for its first visitors.

****

The first landing crews immediately set about demarcating a landing zone for the next wave and erecting the inflatable portable shelters that had been transported down to the surface. Lightweight but durable, each shelter could accommodate several people with rudimentary facilities. They were designed to permit modular expansion with each basic unit being customizable for a more specialised role; command structure, the mess, kitchens, dorms, labs, even manufacturing facilities.

The second wave of landers included Mandy and the first complement of droids who had split into two teams of five (having packed out lander number three to the seams). The first squad was working on assembling one of the two lightweight OEV's that had been stowed under the lander. These were a bare bones version of the same vehicle that Cassus has driven with Brox to Star City with beefed up suspension and bigger wheels. They had no independent life support systems although there was a limited supply of emergency oxygen and other tools and an adaptable flat-bed stowage system at the rear of the vehicle behind the two-man cabin. A third or even fourth passenger could stand or wedge themselves onto the flat-bed if necessary.

The second squad of Mandy's droids had erected an impressive looking industrial 3D printer, which would be run continuously to provide a more permanent base for the Pergans and their vehicles.

*****

Soon there was a rough working base tucked the lee of a small hill on a flat plain in the Northern hemisphere selected for its comparative stability.

"Why didn't we just send the droids down first?" Bronzemerit asked, looking ill at ease in his red Z81 EVA suit.

"We cannot rely on droids. Useful as they are. People need these skills too. Flesh and blood!"

"I agree," said Bronzemerit, "but, we're not actually staying here are we?" he said looking back at the bustling people and droids working side by side in the rapid fabrication process.

"Not this time my friend. It's all just an extended training exercise, but fascinating to think that this is how Acto was founded. This or something quite like it." Cassus mused.

*****

The following day Cassus returned to the moon with the same crew and Kel Fox at the controls once again.

The droid complement under Mandy had remained on the moon and continued to work overnight on the ground base of operations. This had advanced sufficiently to permit extended stays and Cassus intended to spend his first night on Martian soil, leaving Elara in command on the Perga.

It was a short walk from the Landers to the command structure, which was now two storeys tall. Cassus paused as one of the RDG class droids crawled up the nearest façade of the 3D printed structure to the second storey and final level of the building that was still under construction. The last part of this first phase of infrastructure would be the control tower that served the dual purpose of flight control and as a look out post. This central building was surrounded by the modular inflatable shelters and flanked by a small hanger / workshop for the EAV's. Cassus grunted in surprise and even a measure of distaste as the droid continued with its unconventional construction methods and pressed on, towards the main airlock.

An hour later Cassus was joined by some of the senior staff on the command level where he had been pouring over images taken of the moon by the Perga on a holo-projection unit. Large tracts of the moon remained dark where the its rotation had not yet been scrutinized by the orbiting mothership.

Cassus sipped a hot coffee as Eston zoomed in on the area around the operating base and pointed out various geographical features to his assistant Claudia Grace.

Brox, Boomer, Senator Temorri and his aide were also present.

"If we're going to explore the local area, may I suggest here" Eston pointed with a long finger at a nearby ravine.

"We'll take both of the operating vehicles" Cassus instructed. "Eston and myself with one of the science officers and ... who can you spare me Boomer?"

Boomer ran a quick mental check "Triple C has just arrived in the last lander. I can spare her for a few hours. Don't take any chances out there. Check in with control every twenty minutes Captain."

Cassus nodded and checked his suit chronometer, "I'll grab the OEV's and we'll depart at 1400 hours Acto time.

*****

Eston insisted on bringing his personal assistant, Claudia Grace, who also formed part of the Grounds Ops crew.

"You'll have to perch or squat on the back of the OEV Clauds" Cassus warned her.

Clauds nodded "I'll make do". The three of them carried out suit safety checks, paying especial attention to Eston and negotiated the main airlock. The OEV's had both been stowed in the cramped hanger / workshop. Cassus actually had to stoop slightly to avoid hitting the top of his head on the ceiling of the small the hanger, which was deserted.

Cassus checked the OEV over and thumbed the power toggle which showed the battery level to be in the green.

"Brox, you take Triple C and I'll bring Eston and Clauds." Brox gave the thumbs up and Cassus swung himself into the waiting OEV.

Claudia Grace stepped up onto the rear cargo flat-bed and strapped herself to the roll bar. Cassus tried to look around and realised it was impossible in his Z81 extravehicular suit. He frowned in annoyance and checked in with the comms unit instead.

"Snug as a bear chief!" Clauds confirmed. Cassus raised an eyebrow and powered up the vehicle, plugged in the satellite coordinates into its guidance system and headed out, into the unknown, crushing the surface under his heavy tyres.

*****

The rock ravine wasn't high, less than three times the height of Cassus and certainly under 20 foot from the base to the crest but it was extremely rocky, with giant boulders and rocks scattered along its length that ran for several miles according to the orbital data. It was wide enough for one of the lightweight outbound electronic vehicles with some careful driving around, and sometimes through, rock formations that formed fantastical shapes after eons of weathering from dust storms.

Perga Minor was too far out of the habitable zone to have sustained life and unlikely even to have ever had any water deposits. It was as dead and as dry as old bones. It may have been devoid of life but the ravine certainly showed some of the planet's geology and Professor Eston Cousteau was keen to investigate. The entrance to the ravine was only a few miles from the base camp; far enough away to make Boomer, who was serving as head of ground ops, nervous but well inside the operating capability of the stripped down OEV's.

"Wind speed has increased down here Captain," Claudia cautioned.

Cassus checked his visor HUD and the more limited information available on the OEV's dash-controls. He paused wiped some dust away from the dashboard and slowed the vehicle to a standstill, less than one hundred feet into the ravine. The second OEV with Brox and

Sergeant Lowery braked hard behind them, prompting Cassus to think fleetingly about installing some sort of rear brake light for future use.

"We're in operational parameters. No real danger but I think this will do us. Eston, will this work for you?"

Eston gazed around, temporarily lost for words. "So much" he mumbled to himself "so much to discover. What? Oh, yes very good. Tres bien indeed!"

"Claudia, would you mind unloading my equipment please? Oh, you have already!"

After collecting himself and picking through the equipment crates Eston quickly assembled a portable trolley, his hands sure from years of practice, his eyes ranging over his equipment carefully.

"This, yes, this and this. Probably don't need the hygrometer but let's take it anyway. Where are the rock hammers? Claudia, have you seen the rock hammers? They're small hammers."

Claudia smiled and rummaged in another sturdy looking chest and pulled out two wicked looking titanium rock picks and some smaller geologist's hammers and added them to the pile.

Within a short time Eston seemed satisfied and having fixed his eye on a rock formation a couple of hundred meters further into the ravine he moved off with surprising adroitness considering the limitation of the exo-suit.

*****

Almost an hour passed and Cassus, Brox and Triple C wandered back along the ravine to the vehicles stopping occasionally to pick up a curiously shaped rock. Cassus pocketed a couple to take back to Acto. The windspeed within the ravine had picked up and started to lift dust and even small pebbles from the ravine floor and throw them carelessly against the rock walls, albeit without any real force.

Brox looked around anxiously "Not sure I like the wind in here Captain. It's stepped up again. These OEVs are robust enough but they don't offer any protection. Suggest we withdraw."

Cassus had noticed the environmental conditions and agreed immediately. "Call Eston and Grace back to the OEV's and let's get back to base. Sergeant Lowery , can you call in to base please".

Eston and Grace had meandered a couple of hundred meters further down the ravine to inspect some exotically shaped rocks. Brox peered at them though the dust "C'mon, c'mon, check your comms you old fool."

"They're not answering Captain. I don't know if it's interference or what but neither of 'em are responding."

"Eston I can understand. Claudia should know better. Maybe their comm units are out. Let's get down there fast."

Brox and Triple C set off as quickly as they could in the EVA suits with Cassus just behind.

'We've got to improve these suits,' Cassus thought as they lumbered awkwardly towards the silent scientist.

"Visibility is still falling Sir. Helmet torches on everyone," Brox ordered.

Cassus fiddled in mid-stride with the control unit on his wrist and his powerful helmet torch joined Brox and Triple C's, piercing through the murk.

"Thought these things came on automatically?" Triple C queried.

They do. There must still be too much light" Brox replied.

"These suits need a number of modifications apparently." Cassus agreed.

Cassus followed the bobbing light of Brox's helmet ten foot in front of him. "We must be getting close now" came Brox's voice in Cassus's ear. The dust was bone dry but fine and a patina was starting to build on the edges of the wide arc of his visor. This was made of polycarbonate plastic and gold with layers of filters and protection as well as heating systems to clear debris.

Cassus could feel the wind on his chest as he peered down the ravine.

A moment later Triple C spotted the missing duo, "There! 2 o'clock – By that rock. Isn't that Eston's equipment?"

Cassus moved closer, a growing feeling of unease gnawing at his gut.

"Something is wrong" Brox muttered. "Still no comms and they should be able to see us at this distance."

Cassus pressed on, he was on only thirty foot away from a small pile of equipment and a scattering of rocks. He brushed the cloth on the back of his gauntleted hand over his visor and stepped forward into the wind, dust and small fragments of rock hitting his suit.

Brox saw it first.

A gauntleted hand thrust up between a pile of rubble. A rockfall or landslide had buried Eston and Claudia alive.

*****

"Who is it?"

"I can't tell. Al the suits are the same, but I'd say, Eston. Yes, it's Eston. Shit."

Cassus reached the scene and looked around a little wildly inside his helmet, which did nothing at all. Time seemed to speed up exponentially. "Get him out! Where's Clauds?"

In their haste to reach their crew mates no-one had brought tools from the OEV but Eston's equipment included picks, trowels and collapsible shovels. Brox rooted around and threw Cassus a small but sturdy hand shovel. Cassus grabbed the tool from mid-air, dropped to his knees and began digging around Eston's raised fist.

Through the dust and debris Cassus lost sight of time as his world narrowed to a few square feet. Brox and Triple C were working nearby, but Cassus barely registered them as he fought through rock and dust to uncover the buried Scientist.

It didn't take long. Most of Eston's torso was only lightly covered and as soon as his helmet was clear he was able to help his rescuers complete the job.

Cassus checked over his suit, looking for rips or punctures. "Where's Clauds" Cassus cried. Eston shook his head and tapped his helmet, indicating he couldn't hear Cassus, who nodded and pointed to his lips through his visor.

"Where is Claudia" Cassus enunciated clearly. Eston looked around but shook his head again sadly. He pointed to an area several foot closer to the old rock face and shrugged.

"Brox, get him back to the OEV and get him back to base. Check that suit again as well."

"Aye Sir". Brox picked up the battered old man easily and strode away, covering the ground quickly with his long legs.

"Back to it Charlotte – She's here somewhere. If her air supply is intact, she'll still be alive."

In his heart Cassus felt certain that Clauds was alive. She was there, just waiting for them to rescue her so she could get back to the ship and resume her duties. The image of Triple C and Wyles working together in the kitchens flashed randomly across his mind and he reflexively half smiled but them took another look at the landslide and the smile dripped off his face. The debris was deeper closer to the wall of the ravine and huge boulders littered the space. Cassus picked up his tool and Triple C joined him as they attacked the ground with determination.

They worked hard, side by side, sweeping the surface for any sign of Clauds. The ground was unyielding and many of the boulders too large for them to move even working together. They continued regardless, their suits taking scrapes and punishment as they struggled to move hard dead earth and ancient rock. Minutes passed and Cassus soon felt fatigued, sweat running down his brow and prickling against his skin. He set his jaw and persevered. Triple C struggling alongside him.

Soon they were both on their knees, trying to shift rubble away to clear a path. Cassus was quite fit and had a natural strength but he was not used to such manual labour and after ten minutes, physically his body had nothing left to give. His will was stronger though. Harder than iron and as Triple C slumped, exhausted, he crawled on, looking for some sign of his shipmate. He could do no more than paw away the very crust of the earth as his strength failed him.

There was a sound behind him. Growing louder, growing closer. It sounded like marching. Cassus's tired brain groped for an explanation. And then Boomer was there. Massive in his augmented power suit. He towered over Cassus like a colossus as he tossed 100kg rocks around like they were pebbles. Behind him marched Mandy, leading her RDG droids like a phalanx. They looked spindly next to Boomer but their alloys were tougher than muscle and bone and what had started to look like a tomb soon became an excavation.

Cassus was dazed, he struggled to get up off his knees as Boomer passed him at a safe distance working his way to the wall of the ravine. Still there was no sign of his missing crewman. He felt drained, his world had closed in to a small puddle of rock and dust and a single goal of recovery. Moving those parameters was beyond him until he felt many hands upon his person, lifting him up. Boomer issuing orders in his ear but none of it registered. Up he was lifted. Away from the Martian dust of the moon and borne away. "Wait!" he croaked before the last whisper of his strength finally failed and he was carried away, supported by the droids beneath the glowing orb of Perga's dawn. Cassus closed his eyes and listened to the fading sound of debris being tossed aside by man and machine and his heart felt cold. He knew then that Clauds would not be returning to the Perga to continue their mission.

The ravine had become her grave.

CHAPTER 7

Cassus paused outside his door, looking left and right down the corridor. Elara's quarters were just a few feet from his own. He knew she would be there and he took a step towards her door and paused, ran his tongue over his teeth. "Yeah, maybe not today" the Captain said and made the easier decision. He turned and walked away. Towards the droid bay. The Perga had left orbit the day before after an extended stay to pack away valuable equipment and launch a subspace transmitter. The 3D printed core of the base remained intact on the planet. A lonely monument for future travellers.

When he had awoken from his exhaustion, he had sprung up with a frenetic energy; filled with the need for immediate action. His passion was fruitless, there was nothing he could do to change anything and Elara had gently but firmly taken charge of the operation, launching the orbital subspace transmitter to boost communication times with Acto and steering the Perga back into deep space. Cassus had no-where obvious to channel his fervour and had all but shut down for a few days, his mood growing black and dangerous.

He had intentionally sought out Mandy. The cold company of the droid was easier to handle than human sympathy. Easier than being judged.

He absorbed himself in learning more about the droid and her capabilities and spent many hours touring the ship, poking his nose into extremities and the quietest spaces and often visiting her in the droid bay, where the droid contingent remained in their racks, back in eternal slumber until reactivated.

As the days passed other thoughts bubbled to the surface and new channels began to open. These he clung to and poured his time and resource into exploring. The limitations of the Z81 extravehicular suit had tugged at his consciousness even whilst still on the moon and he mused over designs in his head as he pounded the treadmill and pumped iron in the ship's gym. The exercise had the dual benefit of clearing his mind and assuaging the disappointment at his own lack of physical prowess on the surface.

"Have you prepared the new suit Mandy?" he asked as he walked with the droid to workshops in the landing bay.

"Yes. The new prototype has been fabricated by the printers as we discussed. Is that the correct word? Discussed?"

Cassus flicked an eye to the droid, "As good as any I suppose."

"Not ordered? I am fulfilling your wishes but as you made no direct request I thought 'discuss' might be a more appropriate verb."

A faint smile creased Cassus's cheek, "It was a discussion Mandy. You did well."

"But I …."

Cassus clapped the droid on her back and said "Let's park that one shall we?"

"Park?"

"Leave it there. Search your database for 20th century Earth colloquialisms. We're here by the way. Now let's have a look at what you've come up with."

Mandy shook her head slightly, "The human brain works much faster than I had anticipated," she announced and this time Cassus almost laughed.

*****

The armoury was a narrow space with a single high security entrance with a couple of special modifications. The tight space was crammed with racks of weapons and equipment from floor to ceiling on either side of a central corridor. At the front of the bay was a clear area for weapons assembly and inspection with two tables that dropped down from the wall, one on either side of the wall. Two fold-up chairs were also clipped to the wall. A basic but thick metal mesh separated the inspection space from the weapons racks with a security finger pad controlling authorized access.

Brox had lowered one of the tables and sat quietly in the dim light assembling and disassembling a 105E laser assault rifle. The compact assault rifle looked small in his busy hands which moved adroitly over the oiled black weapon. His eyes were on the rifle watching his hands work, but his mind was far away. Back in the dust and rock of Perga Minor.

*****

Sergeant Narcissa was standing less than ten feet away from Brox, tapping her foot impatiently on the deck as she considered how to approach him. One hand rested on her hip, the other poised by the armoury door control.

"Sympathy?" she thought "Not really my strong suit is it. Formal? Try and snap him out of it? Hmm, he's likely to snap back or lock me out altogether. Drinking session? Shag? Damned if I know. Ah, screw it." The Sergeant cleared the door access and stepped into the inspection chamber.

"Hey Brox."

Brox acknowledged her with little more than a grunt but didn't tell her to get lost, which she took as a positive. The quiet was unexpectedly comforting. The firm click and crunch of the laser assault rifle crisp and affirmative. Almost assuring. Narcissa unclipped the second table and pulled out the folding chair.

"May I?" she asked, slightly surprised at herself.

"Help yourself. All the 105's need stripping down."

Narcissa passed through the security door and walked to the end of the rack of 105's. The furthest five were unwrapped and oiled. The sixth was with Brox, the seventh onwards were still wrapped in their crisp protective factory wrappings. The Sergeant hoisted the seventh rifle down from the rack and returned to her station.

The two soldiers sat within a few feet of each other, working quietly and efficiently in the strange peace of the armoury.

An hour passed, then two. With as many words exchanged. The stock of factory wrapped rifles diminished as the time ticked away until there were only a couple left. Narcissa was worried about her friend but had enjoyed the process, which was surprisingly cathartic. After a while she registered that the only sounds were the background hum of the ship and her own work. She felt Brox's eyes upon her. She looked up at him and smiled gently.

Something flickered dimly in his eyes as he looked at her, "We should have brought more rifles" he quipped. "You're good at this."

"Better than talking anyway," she said warmly.

He continued to look at her intently but silently. For once her quick wit failed her. Brox never looked at her like that. Did he?

"Thanks for coming Narse. Appreciate it." He said slowly. "Shall we get out of here?" he asked and she nodded, rose like a cat and took his hand.

*****

"The Proto-type Z82 Captain." Mandy pointed at a workbench upon which lay a nearly complete EVA suit including a modified version of the Z81 helmet.

"All the modifications have been incorporated into this design. So far as the fabrication process allows."

"Does the helmet turn?" Cassus asked as he examined the suit.

"Yes captain, the neck piece has been recast by the Engineering team to allow 180-degree rotation of the helmet."

"Good. What else?"

There is a back-up system for the short-wave radio transmitter in the arm and the chest piece has been reinforced with carbon fibre. It's 17.8 times stronger than the previous design."

"What about the helmet torch?"

"This one's light meter has been recalibrated but you can turn it on from the suit wrist control or manually from the helmet itself."

Cassus nodded, pleased. "Anything else you can think of Mandy – Let me know. I want this suit operational for testing by the time we commence the crew's drills.

We'll discuss those at the briefing. Anyway, it's high time I paid a visit to the bridge."

The droid cocked her head and considered the possibilities. Cassus left her in what looked like deep thought.

*****

The next days passed rapidly as Cassus forced himself back into the routine of life aboard the ship and resumed his duties as Captain. He paced the Bridge, stopping occasionally to peer out at the star-scape. The ship was quiet as Elara had recommenced the stasis sequence a few days following departure from the Perga's Dawn. There were only three other people on the Bridge besides Cassus. The Earth / Acto correspondent Stuart Bronzemerit, Ensign Sal Puar in communications and James Nosse at his Navigation console.

Cassus had asked Bronzemerit for summary of the latest news reports issued from the Perga. The journalist had lost weight whilst onboard and looked perky but he was restless and fidgeting more than normal.

"There's something you're not telling me. What's wrong?" Cassus asked brusquely.

"I haven't mentioned this yet, but it's probably the most important thing." Bronzemerit took a breath and plunged on, "we have a new name for the system Captain."

Cassus cocked his head.

"Er, the system we just left. Where the accident occurred." Stuart clarified.

Cassus smiled faintly and nodded, "I recall it vividly. Go on."

"Well, I asked the crew and the decision was unanimous. I have taken the liberty of logging it already. You will see doubtless see it across the media channels, once they reach us out here."

"What did they decide on?"

"The Claudia Grace system, Captain. I hope that is satisfactory?"

Cassus eyed Bronzmerit for a moment. The journalist looked back a little doubtfully until Cassus clapped him on the shoulder, "it couldn't really be called anything else could it?"

"Do you think we'll go back there one day?" Bronzemerit asked.

"No. Not us anyway. Not on this ship. It's a fitting name though. Thank you." Cassus replied and turned away.

*****

"Sir! There's a message. Priority one. It's from Acto!" Ensign Sal Puar squeaked from her place at the comms station.

Cassus raised an eyebrow and hurried over to Sal's station. The visibly excited young Ensign punched the message onto a viewscreen.

"What's this? Cassus asked trying to decipher the random assortment of words and symbols on the screen

"It's encoded to your private channel Sir. Shall I direct it to your ready room?"

Cassus thought for a moment, weighing matters in his mind but decided not to withhold anything from his small crew. The likelihood was the news would get out anyway and sooner rather than later.

"No, carry on Sal."

The small Ensign looked up, pleased to be included. "Here we go Sir. There are multiple layers of protection. It's a code one from your brother. It's dated from several weeks ago."

Cassus read the message, which unlike VII's normal verbose style was short and to the point. 'Trouble' he thought immediately.

Brother,

I trust the voyage is proceeding as planned. Station Alpha 1 confirmed your safe departure.

The Actavian Security Force recently found an abandoned OEV in a standard sweep outside the city. There was a residual blast patch in the sand which matches the exhaust pattern of two Lynx class engines or equivalent. We believe this to be a small two-man ship capable of limited hypersonic flight. This can only be one man - Governor Sendrick. He did not die on Acto. Lyron will look to use this to his own advantage. I've called a meeting of the Senate and I'll update you when I can.

Vil.

"Well." Said Cassus, "Well, well, well" and he bit his lip.

*****

Vil brooded as the Senate chamber filled quickly to capacity, wishing he was anywhere but here in this magnificent prison. A nervous dread gnawed at him and he needed to piss. He rubbed his temple and thought about his brother's response to his message. The Perga had acknowledged his sub space message faster than anticipated. Cassus had responded with four lines;

Keep Lyron in check. Whether Governor Sendrick lived and escaped or not doesn't change anything. Investigate the archives for any sort of prototype two-man or four-man hypersonic ship. The Perga's mission will continue regardless. I have sent a separate open transmission regarding the tragic death of Claudia. Commemorate her appropriately. I will visit her family on my return.

Senator Lyron and his supporters rapidly filled their benches whilst Vil's cadre of loyalists filled the benches on the opposite side of the aisle. Lyron had many supporters, a number that had grown over the last few weeks as he'd played up his relationship with old Governor Sendrick and cast doubt on the Toradon's legitimacy. They were confident and brash. Lyron was on a roll, his constant barbs regularly striking home. In the last few Senate encounters Vil had generally come off worse in their exchanges in what was known as the 'Governor's Time'. This marked the culmination of the day's debate and some general governance points of order.

The Lyron faction as they had become known, had not made any direct move against Vil's governorship but they were becoming bolder. Lyron had done nothing to discourage the rumours that were circulating of his desire to return power to the people, to redistribute wealth and terminate Acto's nascent deep space industry and divert funding elsewhere.

The final session of the week was drawing to a close and Lyron had centre stage.

"The Perga is too expensive! This deep space crusade was launched off little more than a Toradon's whim! He exclaimed to a spattering of applause. "Whilst I sympathise with the Toradons for the loss of their parents, their position does not guarantee them the right to squander our planets remarkable resources on a rescue mission! A mission that, I am afraid to say, has almost zero chance of success!"

'Bloody politicians!" Vil murmured under his breath.

"The resources wasted on this folly could and should have been used to improve standards here on Acto! The Actavian people are the ones suffering and the Governor and his stand-in," Lyron pointed at Vil airily, "seem to be determined to simply ignore their needs in pursuit of their personal quest for redemption!" The Lyron benches applauded loudly and banged their feet.

Vil flushed, his dismay retreating as quicky as his anger blossomed hot and fast and he shot to his feet. "The Senator is forgetting that *all* these programmes received full approval from the Senate. I'll remind the Senator that this Government is democratically elected by the people that he suddenly seems to be so fond of! I don't recall such deep concern for the Actavians going further back than the last few weeks!" Vil looked around the chamber, "Do any of our long-standing members recall the Senators concern perhaps? Did I miss a communique?" The benches rippled with sporadic laughter from both sides.

"Let me refresh the Senators memory yet further, as he seems to have neglected the huge employment this programme has created. The *boom* in skills we have developed here on this planet – on Acto! The exports that have fed our growth, propelling our standing in the Federation. The Actavians, whom the honourable Senator has seemingly just remembered, have prospered under Toradan guidance. The Senator has taken to recalling tales of the previous Governor and their close relationship. Has he forgotten the forced labour camps I wonder?" Vil pressed on, his voice going in strength. "How convenient for him!" The chamber erupted in a cacophony of noise. Lyron glared at Vil. He would have flicked a forked reptilian tongue out if he'd had one, but it was clear that he was taken aback by this sudden turn of events.

Vil seized the initiative and hammered home his attack, calling for silence or at least some measure of calm, "Yes, yes, there are some who haven't caught up yet, a few who have slipped the net but our work is not yet complete." Vil considered his next works but ploughed on, "I will say here and now for the records that this Administration will not ignore our people. The Senator talks about 'the people' constantly but is not offering any new solutions. Indeed, he appears to be suggesting resurrecting old theories that have never worked. He is neglecting, or has forgotten, the hard lessons of the 20th and 21st Century, the appalling misery and poverty that socialism and unchecked ancient religion engineered. The near disaster of the revisionist third dark age, the crushing puritanical heresy that set mankind back a century! I will remind the Senator of that period! The censorious stalling of progress when a shroud of prejudice, hatred, ignorance and superstition all but killed the free exchange of ideas and shattered the hard-won progress of the enlightenment. As a result, humanity limped into space when it could and should have run. I say to the Senate that we will not return there. Not ever."

Vil paused and took a breath, his mouth dry. "As a great man once said, 'You don't make the poor rich by making the rich poorer' and on this planet, under our guidance, we will not drag people down but rather endeavour to raise everyone up. None will be forgotten." Vil blinked and stopped again as his fervour cooled and looking round the chamber. He was hit by an immense sense of relief in the knowledge that this round at least was almost won. "The Senator can join us in this great period of enterprise if he chooses. Now I will ask my esteemed colleague Senator Rosalind Corn to cover the last item tabled for discussion today, the public ceremony commemorating the death of crewwoman Claudia Grace." He finished quietly and this time the applause came from all sides.

Some particularly noisy cheering and shouts of "Go on Vil! Hurrah for the Governor!" burst from the small public balcony at one end of the Senate chamber. Vil could see Lilia, Greg Milson, Lucinda Grey, Alan Spartan and even Duster crammed into that cramped space. Milson was making the universal 'Let's have a drink' gesture with his fist.

Vil waved cheerily and gave them the thumbs up but sat down heavily, suddenly exhausted. Senator Guy Royal patted him on the back and leaned over, "Well said. You're getting the hang of this now Governor."

Senator Corn had managed to restore a semblance of order although conversations both loud and more discrete still buzzed around the chamber. "Senators! Senators please! I'm sure none of us want to be here indefinitely. We must move on to the final item. Cassus

Toradon himself has sent us a message! I will read it to you now."

Vil didn't hear the message, although he knew the bones of it and had already started making preparations for the day in question but he paid no attention to the rest of the session, his responsibilities fulfilled.

*****

"I want a full weapons test tomorrow Brox and if it's successful we will spend the next week running emergency drills with the crew. Commander Elara, I know you have already prepared some scenarios for us?"

Cassus was in a briefing of the senior officers in his ready room. The entire crew had been pulled out of stasis over the previous week and settled into the increasingly familiar regimen of life aboard ship. James Noose the navigator, chief engineer Pete Marcell, Flight Lieutenant Bob Scholes, Doctor Catlea and Mandy were also present around the command table.

Commander Elara smiled, "We have prepared several scenarios Captain".

Brox leaned forward, planting a chunky elbow on the table. "We're ready Captain. I'm confident all systems are fully operational. What are we targeting?

"We've pulled out of hypersonic flight just a few thousand kilometres from a stable asteroid belt at the edge of this system which the Captain will name after the, ahem, winner of the next Perga games night competition in 3Bar."

The announcement caused several grins from around the table as the serious young man set out some more details concerning their location and risks.

Elara then took over and outlined the first set of scenarios for the week of intense emergency and battle simulations. "The training session will end with a full day scenario between two teams who will be selected by the Captain and myself over the week. This will be a competitive simulation split into two main segments. The morning session will include several objectives in space with most of the Perga's ships taking part in a simulated space battle and defence of the Perga. After a break for lunch we will continue with a scenario which assumes the Perga has been boarded by enemy forces with the crew split between boarders and repellers."

Brox was nodding and looked like he could not wait to get stuck in but there were more sombre faces around the command table.

"I like the idea Captain, I do. It should be realistic, but putting all of our combat ships out at once in an untested environment so close to an asteroid field is risky. I'd prefer an extra day to limit the Ops theatre and put some beacons out to warn our pilots if they stray out of the Ops zone." Scholes advised.

Cassus considered and agreed with this suggestion and several more about improving safety for the pilots including a triple check that sustained hits from the lowest power setting on the laser systems did not actually damage the ships, or the Perga. "All right, Bob!" he said laughing, holding up a hand, "Do what you need to do to ensure the safety of our pilots and the ships. You'd best get started!"

"Is all this really necessary Captain?" The chief engineer interjected. "There's no other sentient life in the Galaxy. Not that we know of anyway. We're not at war with anyone. How likely is it that the Perga, the most advanced ship for light years, is ever going to be under threat?"

Cassus had expected the question from the straight-talking engineer, whose expertise was unparalleled but whose imagination outside the realms of the mechanical was limited. "Bolt, the Perga *is* an incredible ship and you're right in the sense that humanity has yet to find trace of intelligent life. That doesn't mean we're alone, although that's a conversation for 3Bar. The fact is I'd rather prepare for the worst and regardless, it keeps the crew alert."

"Understood Captain." Bolt conceded. "It will help operational efficiency."

"I also want the new improved Z82 suit tested at various points over the week, including Engineering. Mandy will distribute the suits that are available. How many do we have now?"

"We will have enough for all members of the crew Captain."

"Excellent. I want to see how it compares to the standard version. Mandy, select a dozen members of the crew at random to use the Z82 and report on its performance," Cassus ordered and received nods in return from around the table.

"You know, this whole thing will create a lot of injuries and work for my team Captain!" Doctor Catlea put in. "Which, I welcome by the way. I'm getting rusty and bringing Brox out of statis, whilst challenging, isn't what I trained for!"

"Thanks a lot Doc" an indignant Brox said.

Catlea patted the big man on his shoulder.

"You won't have to deal with anything too serious I hope Catlea but inevitably there will be injuries. It will be good for your team to mend a broken bone or two. Who knows how long we're going to be out here!" Cassus winked.

"I'm hoping to get home before we hit old age Captain," Brox rumbled.

"What about the RDG droids Captain? Do you wish them to take part in any of these simulations?" Mandy asked.

"Yes. Prepare half the contingent for the final day and let's see what they can do." Cassus looked around the command table, "It will be an intensive and exhausting week, but I hope the crew can have some fun as well."

"What's the plan once we've completed the drills?'

"We'll be going back in stasis Doc. It's almost time for the next stage of our journey."

CHAPTER 8

Elara's planning was meticulous. Cassus was impressed. The Captain and the Commander were relaxing in 3Bar after the fifth day of drills and emergency procedures. The crew had been offered half a day's leave to relax and after touring the ship with his number two Cassus had asked her whether she fancied a drink. They meandered down to the ship's recreation space on deck three which included the now permanent bar installation. Cassus ordered another beer from acting barman Wyles and Elara was debating the available gin offer, much to Cassus's amusement.

"I think I'll try the wild strawberry and berry flavour please"

"Coming up Commander."

Cassus swigged his lager and waited for the inevitable taste test. A tentative sip. An appreciative little smile "Hmm, not bad," she confirmed. "Not my favourite though."

"What's your favourite El? Let me guess – Rhubarb and Actavian hydroponic generic fruit flavour?"

"No!" Elara laughed, "although you got the Rhubarb bit right. Its Rhubarb and Ginger actually."

"Wait a minute, we've got one of those in stock haven't we?" Cassus said, eyes ranging the selection of drinks behind the bar.

"Yes, but I'm saving that for a special occasion." Elara said wistfully.

"The whole bottle?"

"Well, maybe two special occasions then."

Cassus laughed and pointed to a small booth tucked to the side of bar at the furthest end of the large space. "Shall we?"

"Why not. It's been an exhausting week so far and if I'm honest, I'm nervous about the exercises tomorrow."

"There's an element of risk for sure El. I'm not entirely comfortable with it myself but we can't wrap the crew in cotton wool. They're all competent adults and they all wish to participate. They'll have to step up and take responsibility for at least some of their own decisions tomorrow."

Elara agreed, sipping thoughtfully at her gin. "What about the teams Cassus. Any last min changes?"

Cassus, Elara and a couple of the other senior officers had developed the team sheets over the course of the week as they watched the crew perform. The intention had been to break up the existing cliques, at least to some extent. "Yeah, it's as good as it can be. Brox and Sergeant Lowery from Ship security and Ground Ops to lead team A. They named themselves 'The Raptors'. I say 'they', really I mean Brox." Cassus smiled as Elara raised an eyebrow. "Boomer and Sergeant Narcissa will lead team B".

"And what's their overtly masculine code name? The Predators?"

"Umm, no. I believe they've called themselves the Redoubtables."

"Oh ho! That's not bad. Not bad at all. What about the Senator and his odd assistant?"

"They'll take part. It's compulsory." Cassus sniggered, "although they are on opposing teams. Thought I'd give the Senator a break from her perpetual whining."

Elara snorted. "FJ seems to be determined to participate as well? He doesn't want to adjudicate with us and that creepy droid of yours?"

"He's taking part alright. He thinks it's a colossal waste of time by the way but he refuses to be left out. He's on the defence team under Boomer and Narcissa."

"I'll keep an eye out for him." Elara polished off her drink. "Time for another one Captain?" she asked.

Cassus checked the LCD chronometer on his uniform sleeve. He was enjoying himself and it was early, "I can do one more before we head to bed. Need to be fresh for tomorrow El!"

"We're going to bed are we Cassus? Elara looked inquiringly at him.

A drop of red flushed quickly to the Captain's face but he recovered quickly and smiled her a full toothed smile. "Yes, I'd like that El" he said and this time it was Elara's turn to blush.

*****

Brox, Flight Lieutenant Bob Scholes and Flight Sergeant Hannah Wilson were on a fight-path a few thousand kilometres out from the Perga. Brox and Scholes were piloting the powerful Cohort class fighter, Wilson was commanding a 'Pug' lander to emulate a troop carrier. Wilson was grumpy. Not only had she lost the draw to pilot a fighter but she was expected to steer clear of the combat to focus on the Perga itself and try to dock.

Brox and Scholes would face off against Ensign Fox and Flight Sergeant Jim Wolfe. Brox was itching to get stuck in, "This is the first real ship to ship combat simulation this far into deep space. Ever!"

"Let's make it count commander. Fox and Wolfe are untested but they've both got skills behind the wheel. We'll have our work cut out to get Wilson through to the Perga."

"If you can keep them off me, I might have a chance to dock before the Perga blows me out of the sky." Wilson said as she watched the distant blob of light that she knew to be the mothership.

"It will come down to ship to ship combat," Brox answered. "Stick to the plan we discussed in the briefing." Brox checked his onboard display, "five minutes and counting."

*****

The first exercise of the day would only involve the Perga's pilots. In the event that Wilson was able to dock with the Perga the Raptors would be awarded a number of points, if the attempt was foiled the Redoubtables would win that engagement with further points available for either team if any of the Cohort fighters were knocked out of action. For the duration of the exercise all ship systems would be artificially dumbed down so the Perga would effectively be 'blind' to most of the defined area of operations.

The majority of both teams would watch the action live from 3Bar as Exa and Mandy kept score. The second scenario would play out onboard the Perga itself and would see the Raptors attempting to take control of the ship's bridge and other strategic objectives and would continue irrespective of whether or not the Raptors had managed to dock successfully. The majority of the ship's crew would participate alongside half the ship's activated droids which would be split equally between the teams.

"And three, two, one – We are live!" Unknown to them, their crewmates were cheering in 3Bar or their assigned stations. Brox and Scholes shifted power to their ship's Lynx engines and their glow lit up the stars.

"Stay close Wilson!" Brox directed.

"I'll try!"

Wilson shoved power into her Pug's engines and the squat ship responded, falling into position behind the two fighters.

*****

"Ensign Fox. This is Lieutenant Nosse in Navigation. We have enemy contact. You are clear for launch."

"Acknowledged control. Wolfe, we are cleared for launch. Proceed on heading mark 010." Both ships shot out of the Perga's flight deck and Fox was pressed firmly into her flight seat at the ship accelerated.

"Go go go!" she screeched into her flight helmet.

"Ow! My ears!" Wolfe responded as he took up station on her wing several kilometres away.

"Shit, this is close." He muttered.

"Don't worry Wolfe. The ship's auto collision detection won't let you crash into me. Just stay as close as you can."

Wolf eased in another couple of clicks. "Wish they'd let the flight computer handle this!"

Fox laughed, "That would kinda defeat the purpose of the exercise. Hang in there. You'll be fine. Keep an eye on your display. Contact could come at any time."

Fox knew her flight computer should detect the opposing ships before she could see them but if they came in fast the difference would be measured in micro-seconds. All long-range weapons had been deactivated and with the laser banks set to minimum power they would have to be in visual range to register a hit. The command crew had determined that after three direct hits the fighter would be deemed destroyed and would return to the Perga on autopilot slaved to the mothership's mainframe.

The young ensign scanned her heads up display and peered out of her cockpit in all directions.

"See anything Wolfe?"

"Negative. We're only a few minutes out from the perimeter."

Kel knitted her brow. "They want us out this far. Hmm, they're trying to lure us as far from the Perga as possible. Pull out of hypersonic flight and turn around. Get back to the ship!"

Just as they'd completed their turn a proximity alert buzzed in her ear.

"They're here!" she cried.

*****

Brox and Scholes had escorted Wilson and her Pug as close to the Perga as they'd dared, triggering the Perga's desensitized proximity warning and then doubled back to the perimeter at hypersonic speed and hit the brakes, lurking at a near standstill waiting for Kel and Wolfe to appear.

"I've got 'em on proximity scanner!" Brox said as he searched for visual confirmation with his own eyes.

"There they are! Just starting to turn back towards the Perga," Scholes confirmed and shared his visual with the ship's computer which automatically updated Brox's heads-up display with their coordinates.

"Lock on your targeting computer..."

The two ships launched forward, their heat exchange engines glowing golden with sudden power, like twin mini suns. Kel and Wolfe had completed their turn and ploughed power into their own engines but it was too late.

"Fire!" bellowed Brox and the Cohort's triple laser array burst into life, spewing blue fire.

*****

"Oh fuck- a-doodle-do" cried Kel Fox, as her cabin was bathed in a bright blue glow. "They're right up our arse."

Thud !Thud!

"Your ship has been hit twice by Commander Brox," Exa said smoothly over the comm, as Kel tried to twist her ship away. She threw the agile fighter into a series of loops and dives, constantly changing direction.

"What's your status Wolfe?"

"I've registered one direct hit. Making evasive manoeuvres."

"Split up! It's our only chance!"

"What about Wilson in the Pug?" Wolfe asked as he steered the ship away from his squadron leader.

"Forget her, the Perga can take care of herself."

"Agghhhhh! Balls to this, Scholes is right up my arse!"

"Hang on in there Wolfe. Keep going, and meet at these coordinates." Kel punched a heading onto her ship's screen. "I'll come round on your six and support you.

"What about Brox?"

"Let me worry about Brox. You hang on in there!"

*****

"She's going to swing round to help Wolfe." Brox said, "I'll stay on her."

"Predictable. It won't matter, Wolfe is going down!"

Wolfe was no fool and had notched up many hours of training in the simulator, but Scholes was relentless. Hammering him. He scored a second and soon after a third hit. Immediately Wolfe's fighter was locked down as Exa took control and started to guide the ship back to the Perga. The fighter's emergency lighting system shone bright red to denote its 'knocked-out' status.

"Sorry Kel! I'm done. He was just too close." Wolfe sighed, disappointed. He folded his arms as he sat back in his fighter and watched the action on his ship's screen.

"Don't worry about it. You'll get him next time." Kel reassured her wingman.

"Yeah right," said Wolfe sulkily.

Kel flew erratically, trying to hold Brox off. Her neck was aching from constantly looking around to check his position.

Ensign Kel Fox threw herself into flying her ship, concentrating with everything she had to give. With this increased focus her ordinary cares and concerns were temporarily silenced. Something clicked into place then and for a few moments she felt at one with the machine on some elemental level. Suddenly flying at hypersonic speed through deep space no longer felt like an unmeasurably huge weight, grinding her down. It was just another job, something else to be conquered and mastered. In that brief time, the young officer managed to bring her nose in line with her commanding officer's ship. Flight lieutenant Scholes flickered into sight and for half a second she had a firing opportunity.

*****

"What! Wait. I've been hit!" Scholes cried in disbelief. He'd started to manoeuvre to fall in on Brox's wing and taken his eye off Kel's position. The Fox had darted up under his belly and as she passed behind his stern and fired just three rapid shots, one of which registered solidly as a hit.

"Don't worry, I'm still on her" responded Brox as he spun the fighter, closing in as fast as he dared. Even as he uttered the words, he unleashed a barrage of fire which clipped Kel's fighter on its port wing and scored the third and final hit.

"This simulation is now concluded" Exa confirmed to all the pilots.

"What about Wilson and the Pug?" Brox asked.

The Perga destroyed Flight Sergeant Wilson at close range after scoring three direct hits. She did not succeed with her landing attempt. The final score for this scenario is therefore six hits to four. The Predators win. I will now return all remaining cohort fighters to the mothership."

Brox relaxed, letting the tension drain out his body. It was a comfortable win for his team but he couldn't stop replaying Kel's flying in his mind when for a few seconds it looked as though Kel would escape him. 'That was some real flying,' he said to himself as he watched the stars slip by.

*****

After an hour's break and quick bite for lunch the finale of the exercises got under way, with Cassus instructing both teams for the last time in the Perga's briefing room on deck two.

In time honoured fashion each team member had tied a coloured ribbon around their bicep. Blue for the Raptors and Green for the Redoubtables. A lot of friendly jostling and banter was taking place as well as a few subtle and not so subtle bets and bragging.

Almost forty people filled the space, plus half the ship's complement of droids. Mandy had activated these in the morning and distributed them equally between the teams. Each human and mechanoid team therefore had over thirty players. Cassus, Elara and Mandy would adjudicate with Mandy paying particular attention to the droids' performance and monitor any problems.

"What I am sure will be the highlight of the week will commence shortly!" Cassus was saying. "You all know the drill but for anyone who wasn't listening," Cassus looked hard at FJ and the Senator's aide, Dawn Haran, "the Raptors will continue their role as hostiles who have boarded the Perga. Commander Brox and Sergeant Lowery will lead their assault. The Redoubtables under Boomer and Sergeant Narcissa will attempt to defend the ship. We have designated six tactical objectives to capture or defend. These are as follows; the bridge, the emergency bridge, the armoury, engineering, the medical bay and the flight deck. Remember that capturing or defending the bridge is worth two points! Elara, over to you."

"Just to remind you, the current score is six points to the Raptors and four points to the Redoubtables. This means the boarders only need to take and hold three positions to win or the Bridge and one other objective. No automated shipboard defences are active which means the security doors are not working, with the exception of the labs which are off limits by order of FJ. The sensor pads you are all wearing on your uniforms will vibrate and flash red if you are hit. If you're hit, put your arm up immediately and return to your home zone. You have one hour to prepare. This simulation will last for two hours or until all member of the opposing team are out. Good luck all!"

"Good luck teams. I won't invite questions as time is ticking but remember not to shoot Elara, Mandy or myself as points will be deducted! Enjoy this afternoon and we will see you back at 3Bar this evening for drinks."

The crew cheered. The recently awakened RDG droids remaining immobile until the team leaders led them to their respective home starting zones. The Raptors from a docking bay towards the stern of the ship and the Redoubtables in 3Bar, just below the bridge at the prow of the ship.

*****

Boomer and Narcissa were crouched in the main corridor on level three, outside 3Bar. The shipboard lights had been dimmed and the utilitarian corridors around the ship felt alien and menacing. The whole team were packed behind them. They were keen but noisy. Narcissa thought she could hear someone giggling.

"Shut your mouths!" Boomer hissed violently.

She had heard definitely heard giggling. "Remember the plan. After we've taken the bridge and the emergency bridge we split the platoon into two sections. You make for medical; I'll make for the armoury. We'll join up again outside the flight deck and assess next steps." Boomer summarized their plan.

Narcissa nodded then remembered that Boomer might not be able to see "Affirmative. I'm sure Brox will take the armoury. I can't see him bothering with medical."

Boomer grunted. "It's as good a plan as any. You ready?"

"With this rabble behind us what could go wrong?" Narcissa jerked her thumb at the team. She saw the miner's surprisingly white smile in response. "At least we haven't got that old codger FJ" he said. The dark-skinned sergeant frowned. "Oh, he's alright really. He volunteered. I reckon you might stand a chance again him though." Boomer smiled again "Let's keep the Professor where he can't do any damage" Boomer said, referring to Eston Cousteau.

"Yeah, like that's going to happen. Let's move out."

The Redoubtables had four trained soldiers; Corporal Abel Harris and Privates Ryan Vale and Mozz Dering plus Narcissa herself. All of the officers and non-commissioned officers present has received basic weapons training. This included Kel Fox, Sal Puar, James Nosse, Wolfe and Chief Technician Bancroft from the flight deck. After reaching the bridge, the platoon would split. Boomer would take most of the professionals in his section with the remainder under Narcissa as they attempted to take control of the medical bay.

The bridge and its emergency back-up were deserted as expected. It took them several minutes to reach it from the lower deck. Longer than it should have done as Eston's speed on the march was lamentable.

"Another two points to the Redoubtables!" Narcissa laughed. "This is easy!" Wyles opined.

"Easier than it should be yes" Narcissa replied.

"Maybe he's lost?" said Doctor Andreas.

"Nah, don't underestimate the Commander. He'll have a plan."

The main view screen in the bridge lit up with a graphic of the latest score which was then recited verbally by the ship's computer.

"Where are they?" Boomer asked as the scores remained static on the screen. "Seven to six to us" Narcissa said to herself.

"Vale is your squad ready?"

Private Ryan Vale had been assigned to command the droid squad in Narcissa's section. He looked a little bemused. "Well, they can keep up with us. They don't say much though!" Narcissa smiled at the irony of the recalcitrant droids being led by one of the most talkative members of the crew.

"Think we should give them Las-rifles?"

Vale pulled a face. "I guess. I don't think we should have given the Professor one though. No disrespect Sergeant. I meant Eston by the way."

Narcissa nodded. "I gathered that Private. I'll want a report on their performance by tomorrow." The sergeant paused, "and make sure you send a copy to Mandy as well."

Vale saluted, a little jauntily. Narcissa shook her head slightly and turned to Boomer, who was pointing beefy fingers at his own squad leaders.

"Ready to roll Boomer."

"Good luck Sergeant" the asteroid miner replied. "Check in every few mins."

Narcissa nodded and checked her holographic schematic of the Perga. Without another word she set off towards medical, her section hot on her heels, the RDG droids clanking along behind with Ryan Vale bringing up the rear.

*****

Narcissa crouched a few feet from the medical bay. Like many of the Perga's main facilities there were at least two exits but the double doors on level three were the main entrance.

"It's quiet!" Vale whispered.

"Too quiet maybe?"

Suddenly there was a crash from behind. Narcissa and Vale spun round, raising their laser rifles. Professor Eston Cousteau was in the process of picking up his 105, barrel first, aided by Stuart Bronzemerit who seemed to have discarded his own rifle somewhere and was filming and speaking rapidly into a micro-recorder. The Professor looked sheepish and mouthed 'Sorry' to Narcissa, who shook her head incredulously.

Vale had resumed his position, covering the medical doors. His droid squad in identical crouches, silently facing forward.

Narcissa hefted her 105 rifle and peered down its sights, her heart rate elevated. The seconds ticked past but the silence was undisturbed.

"Boomer, come in. We're in position outside medical. Do you copy?" Narcissa spoke quietly into the comms unit on her sleeve.

The comms crackled slightly as Boomer responded "Copy that. You've moved fast. My section is in position outside the armoury. Move out on a count of ten…"

Narcissa and Ryan Vale notified their squads as the countdown continued. "Three, two, one, Redoubtables - Attack!"

"Woot!" Ryan exclaimed. "Attack!" Narcissa yelled, all pretence at stealth discarded. The section shot forward, led by the RDG droids. They were surprisingly quick on their thin mechanical limbs. The first members of the section burst through the medical bay doors; weapons raised. Narcissa's finger reached for the trigger. She frantically scanned the bay, her rifle barrel tracking left then right. It was empty.

"Watch those exits!" she ordered Vale, who motioned to four of his droids and split them off to cover the far door leading to the stasis chamber and the remainder to another door that lead to small series of examination rooms, stores and the Doctor's tiny offices before rejoining the main level corridor.

"There! There, at er, 3 o'clock! Possibly." Bronzemerit pointed, still busily filming. One of the Raptors sprung up from cover behind the deserted medical reception and peeled off a few shots, knocking out two of the RDG droids before diving through the nearer exit, that had been opened by a teammate.

"I think it's Lowery" Vale shouted excitedly, his young eyes picking out the older man. Before he'd finished speaking his rifle erupted in laser fire, which crackled loudly in the confined space. Several other members of the section also started firing wildly, filling the chamber with green laser fire and noise.

"Woah, woah! Cease fire!" Narcissa shouted as her comm unit came to life again. "Sergeant, we have secured the armoury. Report." Boomer sounded urgent.

"Standby!" Narcissa responded as several members of her team rushed past her.

"Where do you think you're going? Professor! Eston – Stop! Senator - Halt!"

Eston either didn't hear or didn't want to as he whooped and hollered, brandishing his rifle like a savage. Senator Temorri was a little slower though and Narcissa's cry drew him back.

"Idiots!" Ryan Vale exclaimed, rolling his eyes. "Um, not you Senator." Drawing close to Narcissa the young private attempted unsuccessfully to lower his voice, "Even the droids know better. Er, maybe." The RDG's had indeed remained stationary. The droid that Sergeant Lowery had 'shot' remained on the deck, one hand raised straight up, it's exterior lights flashing red.

Narcissa was about to order Vale to go and retrieve the other half of the section when the sound of laser fire erupted once again.

*****

"Boomer, I've lost half the section. They ran off and got taken out by the Raptors. I don't think Brox is going for the points. He's kept his platoon together. We've had to fall back towards the armoury.

"Copy that Sergeant. He knows we're here though. A scout ran off as we arrived. Regroup at the flight deck – There's more room. We'll get pinned down in the armoury as there's only one exit. How many men do you have left?

Narcissa grimaced. Only Bronzemerit had re-emerged into the medical reception, running and grinning. The grin quickly disappeared when he'd seen Narcissa's face. The normally easy-going sergeant was not pleased and she continued to scowl, "I've got Vale, Bronzemerit, and five droids. We're on level seven. Lost Temorri a minute ago. Indeed, the Senator was sitting on the deck just around the corner.

"They're coming Sergeant!" He said, despite having been knocked out and ostensibly out of the game. He should have returned to the home zone but had obstinately hung around.

"We've got company Boomer! See you on level nine. Out."

Narcissa peeked around the corner of the junction, "Senator, see if you can slow them down. Er, maybe lie across the corridor or something?"

"This is very tiring work Sergeant!" The Senator saluted and sprawled across the corridor.

"They're advancing Sergeant!" Vale was in a crouch. "Stay down Senator!" He fired off a couple of shots above the Temorri's head and retreated round the corner to join the rest of the section. He checked his rifle's battery and nodded, satisfied.

"The Senator's alright really isn't he?" he said.

A few rifle shots hit the bulkhead as Narcissa's section retreated but the fire was cautious, perhaps wary of hitting the prone Senator. The Raptors advanced slowly but advance they did.

*****

Laser fire followed the retreating Redoubtables all the way to the flight deck but the rest of the section arrived safely. Narcissa was breathing heavily, Bronzemerit was panting.

"Looks like Boomer's section just got here. Oh goodness, I need to hit the gym" the journalist said doubled over, wheezing.

The remainder of the Redoutables were taking up defensive position. Ryan Vale had the rear-guard and shouted over his shoulder "They're almost on us. I can hear them coming!"

"Get two of those RDG's on the door – Quick. Rest of you, on me!"

Narcissa could see Boomer waving as she ran over to one of the open workshop pits with her remaining team members; Vale, Bronzemerit and three of the droids. The six of them barely had time to take cover when the Raptors burst through the doors, deploying into a skirmish line and firing as they came. The rear-guard droids had already been blasted and shoved out of the way. Their external body lights flashed red.

"Did those droids even fire?"

Ryan Vale peered over the top of a large mobile tool station, "Doesn't look like it. Exa or Mandy will know. Speaking of which, look up there!"

Narcissa glanced up and there in the control room she could see Cassus, Elara and Mandy. Cassus waved cheerily. Narcissa flicked him the bird and grinned. Cassus didn't look best pleased. 'Oops' she said to herself. Boomer's section began to return fire. There was barely one hundred feet between the rear of the fight deck and the workstations and the distance between the teams was narrowing quickly.

Sergeant Narcissa shot, ducked, rolled and shot again. "Ha!" she said in satisfaction as Medical orderly Tubb

Kendrick's sensor pad turned red. He stuck his hand up and retreated.

"Got another one!" Vale shouted and one of Brox's droids went down but Bronzemerit was out. The sensor pad on the chest of his uniform flashing red. He'd take the opportunity to discard his rifle, pull out a snack and start filming again; from a safe distance. Some of Boomer's crew were hit as well and were leaving the theatre of combat, hands held high.

"Wow, this is intense." Narcissa breathed.

"It's over. There's too many of them," Ryan Vale said, a bit squeakily.

Narcissa ducked down again as a volley of laser fire flew just a few inches from her head. "Let's go out in style shall we?" and in a few words she outlined her plan.

"I like it Sarge!" the voluble Vale agreed.

"RDG 4, can you push this crate that way" Narcissa pointed in the direction of Brox's skirmish line.

"Affirmative" the mechanoid responded and it began to push the heavy tool station from the side, with Narcissa, Vale and RDG 8 still crouched behind it. Vale began to laugh as he scuttled along bent over double.

"This is actually fun!" he said and Narcissa chuckled, shaking off the tension that had been building up in her shoulders.

The moving tool-station naturally attracted a lot of fire and RDG 4 was soon out of the action. The heavy mobile cover rumbled to a halt.

"This is it then eh! Ready Vale?"

"Most definitely. RDG 8 go get 'em! Don't stop for anything!" Vale commanded the last droid which paused for a moment, head inclined, and then walked straight towards the skirmish line.

"Ummm, what's it doing?"

"Fire at them RDG 8," Narcissa commanded but the droid's 105 rifle remained static at its side. Within a second or two the droid had been hit several times and its emergency lights blinked red, but it kept on going.

"Weird," said Vale who nonetheless jumped out behind the droid and was promptly hit in the face. "Ooh! That tingles."

You're out Vale! Someone roared from the line of advancing Raptors, now almost within spitting distance. Narcissa let off a shot, pivoted on her heel and pulled the trigger a second time but felt two light impacts on her uniform, which lit up.

"You too Narse. Wait a minute, what's this stupid droid doing? Get out of here metal for brains.

"Hey! Stop!" Brox yelped as the RDG stopped in front of him and then picked him up.

****

"Put him down!" Narcissa ordered RDG 8, which held Brox tightly with one metal hand at arms-length. The big man was a foot off the deck. Brox grappled with the mechanical but couldn't release its grip. The RDG unit remained stationary. It couldn't display emotions on its utilitarian face plate but if it could Narcissa thought it would have look puzzled.

"Put. Me. Down! You, you walking scrap-box!" Brox huffed and strained his trunk like arms, shifting his grip to try and dislodge the droid, which wobbled but wouldn't release him.

Narcissa smirked and went to assist Brox but Mandy, flanked by Cassus and Elara, arrived from the control room first. Mandy moved swiftly, almost languidly, covering a lot of ground without any apparent effort. She put a shapely arm around the RDG, which looked primitive and boxy in comparison, and fiddled with a control under a plate on the back of the droid's neck.

After a moment the unit powered down, its lights fading to dark. Mandy manually prised open its fingers and Brox, genuinely angry, dropped with a heavy thump to the ground. He sprang straight back up and grabbed the deactivated droid, flinging it as hard as he could. The unit was freakishly strong and solidly built but without a will to resist, the Commander's throw smashed the lifeless machine against the tool station several feet away.

"Piece of shit," Brox spat and stepped forward, his cheeks flushed, fists clenched.

A hand appeared on his shoulder. Cassus had to reach up but he gripped the Commander firmly. Brox turned his head and glared but his fire quickly cooled and he slumped slightly.

"I think you got it." Cassus said to him, still holding his shoulder as Mandy retrieved the machine.

"So... scrap-box? That's a new one" Cassus said.

"Er, it was all that came to mind" Brox grumbled but he started to smile. The captain called to Mandy, "I want a full diagnostic on that unit and all the droids Mandy. We can't have these things running rogue."

"I have already commenced those programmes Captain. I have ordered all units to return to the droid bay for further analysis."

Cassus released Brox and waved her on. He watched her thoughtfully as she carried the droid silently from the flight deck. Brox interrupted his musing. "At least we won. Ha!"

"Yo Narse, the Raptors knocked your whole platoon out. You lost!" He grinned mightily and, anger swiftly forgotten, bounded over to Narcissa and Vale. He shook the smaller man's hand in a beefy paw and wrapped Narcissa into a hug. Somewhat surprised she nonetheless hugged him back, wrapping herself around him.

"Well played you dirty scoundrel" she laughed in his ear and he squeezed her hard.

CHAPTER 9

After the success and evaluations of the simulations and the grand-finale aboard the Perga, Cassus had permitted the crew a few days to relax before the next stasis cycle. Half of them needed a day to recover from their hangovers following the party in 3Bar and various private parties afterwards. The Perga had returned to hypersonic flight with Exa in control and Elara in command. Cassus wanted to use the time to catch up with some of his other duties and his first stop was the Stuart Bronzemerit's cabin, which doubled as the ship's news centre.

The head of communications to the world outside the kilometre long Perga lived in a triple suite of rooms on the sparsely populated passenger deck on level one. He had a tiny bedroom with a shower. There was a living area with a basic food refresh station and a much larger ready room that had been turned into what Cassus thought looked like a shambolic mess. Two big comfortable artificial leather chairs were stationed by a large desk that sat flush against a wall. It was littered with various devices, screens, keyboards, data pads and various recording equipment. Cassus recognized an early Star City promotional poster featuring the Perga on one wall and several empty nutriboosts and crisp packets in various nooks and crannies.

After declined the opportunity for an interview (again) both men had settled into the chairs.

"You should look at this Captain." Bronzemerit pressed a button on the portable device in his hand and a large three foot wide pop-up screen appeared. Text and video messages flowed rapidly across its surface. Cassus moved closer to inspect it as the journalist rummaged around for a snack.

"What are these? Messages from the Actavians?"

Bronzemerit smiled. "Not just Acto. These are messages from the whole Federation." The screen continued to scroll.

"Looks like we've received more than a few?"

"There are tens of thousands of them. I've barely scratched the surface. The people are watching Captain."

"May I?" Cassus asked the Terran who had retrieved a half-eaten packet of crisps from a compartment on his arm rest.

"Of course, Captain. Help yourself."

Cassus stopped the display with one finger and hovered over the selection of messages, videos and recordings which were displayed on the screen as pictorial icons with some basic information listed underneath. He selected one at random and a video recording of a young girl from Earth appeared immediately on the screen. She was freeze framed in what looked like a small garden and appeared to be around ten or eleven years old. Cassus hovered over the bottom of the screen and hit play.

'Hi, this is a message to Captain Toradon and all the crew of the Perga. My name is Alisla Green from Earth. My family and I have been watching all the news and at school we have a huge map of the galaxy that shows your position. If you get this message I wondered if you could tell me whether it's scary out there in space and if one day you will visit us on here on Earth? I'd love to see the Perga IRL. PS – Do you have any animals aboard? Bye!'

Cassus watched the screen as the girl waved to the camera and the recording ended. "What's IRL? Oh, in real life." Bronzemerit nodded.

"How do I send a response?"

Bronzemerit deposited his crisps carefully and leaned over the captain to adjust some controls. He showed Cassus how to send an audio or video response and reminded him to smile.

Cassus thought for half a minute and hit record. "Hi Alisla, this is Captain Toradon. Thank you for your message, which our Head of News brought to my attention. I am so pleased that you have been following our progress at your school. You won't receive this message for several weeks but we're already further into deep space than any human has previously travelled. It is a bit scary and dangerous but it's also exciting and a real privilege for me to be part of this mission, not just for my home-world on Acto but on behalf of all mankind. I don't have any plans to visit Earth anytime soon but I hope you will be able to visit us when we return to Acto. PS – We don't have an animals but that is an excellent idea for future missions!" Cassus waved and ended the recording.

Cassus sent the recording and sat back in his chair. "I suppose we'd better make an effort to get back to Acto now eh?"

Bronzemerit laughed hesitantly. "Probably for the best. You wouldn't want to disappoint her!"

"Stu, when we get back to Acto I'd like to invite her and her family to visit us. All expenses paid. Perhaps we could invite some other children from Earth and across the rest of the Federation? Maybe some kind of competition?"

"Leave it with me Captain. I've actually already started work on something similar!" Bronzemerit said, delighted. Cassus shot Bronzemerit an approving smile.

"Whilst you've got me, could you show me some of your broadcasts?"

The journalist eagerly punched up a record of his work, expecting to keep the Captain for perhaps ten minutes but for the next hour Cassus read or scanned through the crew interviews, videos and weekly briefings that Bronzemerit had prepared and broadcast from the Perga.

Cassus rolled his tongue along the inside of his mouth, "This is good work. I'm sorry Stu. I have not paid enough attention to this side of the mission. I had no idea that we would generate such interest. You've been busy. You need a bigger team. We'll get it right for you next time. Oh, and let me know when you want me for that interview." Cassus leaned in and clasped Stu's hand briefly but firmly and left the cabin. The door hissed shut behind him.

The veteran journalist watched the Captain leave and then shuffled forward on this chair to replay the Captain's message again. Surrounded by hundreds of thousands of messages from across the populated Galaxy, deep in unknown space, the Perga blazed a path ever onwards. Bronzemerit settled deeper into his chair and watched the screens. They brimmed with messages of encouragement and support and most provoking of all, a clear message of hope for people. He sat and thought and was not unmoved. As he replayed the Captain's message once again to his great surprise a tear rolled down his cheek.

*****

The next couple of days passed quickly, with an endless stream of matters that needed attending to but Cassus revelled in it, his understanding of the ship and her crew improving constantly. The next period of stasis was only a day away. This would be the longest yet, eventually including the entire crew with two officers woken up intermittently to check ship systems. Only Mandy would remain active for the full period.

Cassus had three items on his agenda for the final day before stasis. An hour with the science team, some final safety checks with Elara, Exa and Mandy including the launch of the next subspace transmitter and the crew briefing. The afternoon and evening were completely free but it was becoming a pre-stasis tradition to have a special meal in the ship's dining hall on level four. This feast was prepared by Triple C and her normal contingent of volunteer sou-chefs.

Cassus had finally completed his first interview with Bronzemerit the previous day. As soon as the subspace transmitter had been launched that message would be flung back towards the Claudia Grace system and across the many miles to Acto and its burgeoning Emprise News Station and then beyond.

The captain reached the science complex on level 5 and popped out his ID to gain access through the double set of security doors. Cassus and Vil had both been worried that FJ would somehow manage to blow up the lab and extra safety measures had been taken. A strategy that FJ had wholeheartedly supported.

"Good morning Science bods!" Cassus exclaimed, making Lisa Tyne almost fall off her stool. The science officer had a short blond bob and dainty nose. She was attractive and curvy beneath her tight-fitting white lab coat. She played up her natural giddiness because she thought it was endearing and in truth Cassus did find it endearing, despite knowing that she was in top one per cent of graduates from the Acto academy and in possession of an intuitive and powerful brain. She had known FJ and other eminent members of the science community on Acto since she was very young and had spent her holidays and free time at Star City where FJ had become her mentor and perhaps more Cassus occasionally thought.

"Captain! You made it!" she said happily, "Come in, come in. Can I get you anything?" Lisa bustled around excitedly, clutching a petri-dish containing some reddish looking soil.

"Coffee please Lisa." Cassus motioned at the dish, "Found anything?"

Lisa spun on her heel, torn between the refresh station and talking science. Science won. She thrust the petri dish at the captain who looked at it a few inches from the end of his nose.

"It's dead Captain! A barren rock. No life there at all!"

"On Perga minor I assume?"

"Of course! No life there at all. At least not in the region we visited. We have so much data to analyse!" Tyne trembled as she thought about the reams of data to wade through.

"Ah ha! The Captain has bestowed his mighty presence upon us mortals!" FJ arrived in the main lab from an antechamber.

"Morning FJ. Lisa was just telling me about the data."

"Did she mention how much data there is? Even with Exa working with us every day we receive more than we can hope to even glance at. It's marvellous, but it's frustrating. I need a bigger team Cassus. A much bigger team!"

"Hmmm, I'm getting that a lot recently."

"This ship, marvel that she is, is rammed to the gills with weapons and goodness knows what else when we could have research labs and scientists! There's already enough raw information here to keep a team busy for years even working with a computer like Exa. I need a dozen Miss Tynes. Two dozen Tynes!"

"There'll be another mission FJ. Maybe as soon as next year or the year after. You've got a place on the crew if you want it. We'll talk about the team later. I'll lend you Mandy this afternoon to help with some of the analysis. Best I can do for now."

"Thank you Cass... I mean, Captain. Yes, yes that would help actually." FJ wondered off, already thinking about the tasks he could assign an RDX class droid to.

Cassus watched him fondly. "So, how about that coffee Lisa?"

*****

After the evening meal Cassus retired with Elara to his quarters. The two of them were spending more time together since the accident and Cassus found that he increasingly enjoyed the petite woman's company although neither of them had yet talked about what it was they were actually doing.

"So, we'll be in stasis for a month, revived for a few days for exercise and nutrition and then back into stasis for the final month. Then we'll be close to this keplar planet you want to visit?"

"That's right El. It's a planet in a 'K class' solar system. It's in the sweet spot of the habitable zone and is the most likely destination for my parents."

Elara thought for a moment and reached out to take Cassus's hands. "What if there's no sign of them Cassus?" she said gently. "Do we carry on? We'll have been out here for more than six months by the time we reach the system."

Cassus looked at her and pondered. "Coffee?" he said.

"Decaf please. It's too late for a stimulant."

Cassus smiled, a crude retort on his lips but held himself in check. He brought the hot drinks back to the table and sat down. "The truth is, when we set out I had thought about just carrying on El. Even if Keplar is as dead as they rest of the galaxy, I had a mind to just keep going." Cassus rubbed the rim of his mug with his thumb, "After Claudia Grace I didn't have any intention of going back to Acto any time soon. If at all."

Elara sipped her decaf and watched her captain, now lover. "I thought so. We could you know? The crew will follow you. I don't believe anyone has even thought about turning back yet."

"They will. Everyone knows or has guessed by now that this is the system I wanted to reach. There are few secrets with a crew of this size."

"I wonder what we will find out here," Elara pondered.

"Hopefully something. The science teams have already told me they've got enough new data to last them for years but I'd like to take something back, even if it's not my parents."

'It's already been a success Cassus," Elara said taking the captain's hand. You've already accomplished much just by being out here."

"I know, but if we can do something spectacular, we might galvanize the rest of the Federation back out into the unknown."

"This mission is far from over. Come on, I've got another mission for you tonight. Can you boldly go where few men have gone before?"

Cassus grinned and said 'Few?" which earned him a scowl and then he allowed himself to be led to his bedroom.

*****

"We are now moving into high orbit around Keplar 442b. All systems are normal." Exa announced to the bridge crew.

The double stasis cycle was complete. Almost three months had passed since the Raptors had declared victory and the Perga sped on, reaching its highest speed yet. A colossal distance vanishing behind the steady power of its Panther class engines. The ship had started to slow the previous day and cruised into the system earlier that day, eventually taking up orbit around their destination.

"What do you say Pergans? Time for a proper look at this planet?" Cassus asked. The bridge was crowded. Several teams had found some spurious reason to be there, including the science teams.

The Captain intentionally kept the main view screen off although he strongly suspected that some of his colleagues had taken a peek as they'd approached the planet from their bridge stations. There was an undercurrent of good-natured excitement. Cassus had the peculiar sensation that his crew were pleased for him.

"Punch it up Exa!"

The planet swam into view beneath them. It was much larger than Acto and larger than Earth, classified as a 'super Earth'.

Time seemed to hang in suspension for a moment and then reality crashed back in and a moment of absolute silence as their eyes drank in the view which was rudely interrupted by a cacophony of sound. A rush of exclamations and a dozen conversations. Cassus stayed quiet, aloof. He continued to watch the viewscreen as the planet rotated beneath them.

It was green.

The land was a mottled green and red and dotted with what could only be several seas beneath a cloudy atmosphere.

"Exa, report on planetary statistics."

"Keplar-442b is approximately 2.3 earth masses in the habitable zone There is minimal axial tilt with a circular orbit around the star of this K-type extrasolar system. It orbits its star every 112 days and receives over 88% of sunlight compared to Acto, being 70% of the sunlight received compared to the Earth. This is a tidal planet on a long term stable orbit around its Star. Initial scans show a breathable atmosphere and considerable flora and fauna with evidence of multiple fires and smoke which would suggest a form of intelligent life… "

Cassus drew in breath sharply and missed the rest of the report as he was suddenly mobbed by his crew.

Eston was beaming and bouncing on the spot, FJ was thumping him weakly on the back. Brox was shaking his hand with Narcissa leaning into him. Elara was a short distance away, smiling with something like joy tinted with relief. "I told you so!" she mouthed at him. Bronzemerit was uttering mild profanities and Senator Temorri was shaking his head. Boomer stood a little distance away, a silent hulk but he was smiling. Mandy watched this display of human emotion closely from her station.

"Congratulations Captain, you have discovered life." Exa stated.

*****

The enormity of that statement hit Cassus like a battering ram but he tried to stay calm. To set an example to the crew. After shaking several hands and even accepting a few hugs he called for calm and started to issue orders to settle the crew down through the medium of work.

Cassus grabbed the comm and issued a ship-wide broadcast. Everywhere, members of the crew who hadn't found a suitable excuse to visit the bridge stopped what they were doing and listened.

"Good morning Pergans. This is the Captain speaking. I wouldn't mind betting that most of you have already heard the news. We arrived in this K-type system a few hours ago and have entered orbit above 442b. This planet is in the habitable zone and our initial scans show that there is a breathable atmosphere and indication of life on the surface. I will schedule a briefing with the command crew this evening and there will be a full crew briefing tomorrow. Watch your comm units for an invitation. This has never happened before and we must make suitable preparations. Once we're ready, a landing party will be selected and we will launch to the surface."

*****

The senior officers and other specialists were seated in the briefing room at the rear of the bridge. All of them had visited the refresh station on their way in. Cassus and Elara had arrived ahead of schedule to discuss the agenda. Brox, Boomer, Scholes, Bolt, Doctor Catlea, Professor Eston and FJ as well as Bronzemerit and Mandy had also been invited to attend. Lieutenant Nosse had the bridge with Ensign Sal Puar.

They'd been ensconced in the briefing room for half an hour already. Everyone wanted to know the plan but as yet Cassus didn't have one. All he knew was the importance of getting it right.

Brox was impatient to get down to the surface, supported by Bronzemerit who could smell a story that would ensure the legacy of them all. FJ and Eston were burning with curiosity but due scientific process curbed their ardour sufficiently to add to the discussion.

"If there is intelligent life down there then we have a moral obligation. This could be first contact between two sentient species," Eston said.

Bolt interrupted, "Pardon me Doc but that's a mighty big assumption. The imaging we've seen so far doesn't show any physical structures. There are no power sources beyond the fires we've seen on the scanners and those could be a geographical phenomenon.

"I said sentient, not advanced. From the evidence we have thus far I would wager we're looking at a preindustrial lifeform, perhaps one living under the canopy of the vast forests we can see below us."

The discussion went on until Cassus called for quiet. "We do have responsibilities. Whether it's a beetle or a bear down there, we must tread lightly and remember it is not our World, but we also have a responsibility to explore, to learn and expand the sum of our knowledge. We can shed light where there was only darkness. Let's say there's intelligent life down there in one shape or another. We need to meet it, not shy away from it. The easier choice is to remain ignorant and that is not the purpose of this mission." Cassus coughed self-depreciatingly, "which of course has er, more than one goal!"

"What about the Planetary Network regulations on first contact?" Temorri put in. He was leaner and looked ten years younger, almost a new man.

Cassus leaned forward, hand on his chin. "I've read those regulations and they are not entirely daft but they were written in a different age. Has anyone dusted them off in the last fifty years? There simply aren't any ships flying outside the long-established trade and passenger routes of the core worlds."

"They're still legitimate," Temorri insisted.

"The governing council on Earth will almost certainly raise them," Bronzemerit put in.

"Only if we tell them," said Boomer. "Why should we? The Federation is a joke. A bunch of red tape bureaucrats lining their own pockets and pretending to have some sort of moral superiority over the rest of us. They have no idea what it's like out here. Why are they relevant to us? They're not. Screw 'em."

Cassus looked at the asteroid miner in surprise. It was the longest speech he'd ever heard from him.

"We cannot willingly turn our back on the Federation and lose the support of the Council on Earth or the other major systems!" Temorri argued. "Acto still has a duty to the Federation!"

"Gentlemen! I'm not so sure we would lose all support if we went our own way but that's not on the table for today. I want to review these rules again before we decide how we're going to interpret them. However, we're all agreed that if there is life, we need to approach it sensitively and not just for the sake of whatever is down there."

Eston agreed enthusiastically, "We don't know how fragile their eco-system is. We cannot permit an invasion of people to this world. We cannot allow it to be exploited and spoiled. It must be protected, not plundered by the other colonies or the Federation!"

"I don't think there will be any plundering Eston. Not by the Federation at any rate. We're a long way from Earth."

"We're a long way from anywhere Cassus!" FJ remarked.

Cassus leaned back thinking. He looked at Elara sitting next to him, her thigh almost touching his. "Thoughts El?"

The petite blond considered her words. "No-one has been in this situation before. We must proceed carefully. I want to set a precedent that others can follow regardless of what the Regulations say. I agree with Eston that this extraordinary planet must be protected, regardless of whether there's sentient life or not, but if there is, we have to respect it and not try and interfere. Does that make sense?"

Eston waved his index finger. "If it's there and we meet it, we will by definition be interfering. Any encounter cannot help but influence the lifeform. We could take another route and observe from afar."

"That would take a more patient, probably better, man than me Professor. We will explore, meet whatever is down there, face to face". Cassus decided. "Stu, if we find sentient life, I want to keep that to ourselves, unless otherwise cleared by myself and only myself. You'll have more than enough to keep you busy anyway." Bronzemerit opened his mouth as if to reply but acquiesced, shrugging "Fair enough Cap'n".

"Bolt – Can you organise a transmitter launch and we'll get a message through to Acto with a code one to my brother. We're going to launch the Pugs tomorrow. Now let's look for a suitable landing site. Exa, display latest orbital imagery please."

A large 3D topographical map appeared on the briefing room's interactive table. The command crew leaned over it, pointing out various details. Cassus zoomed in on the area with the most complete set of images taken from the Perga. These displayed an immense area of forest close to the shore of a small inland sea.

"Overlay sites of recorded fire signatures" Eston instructed the ship's Titan class computer and several dozen pinpricks of fire appeared on the map.

"We should set up a base here," Boomer pointed at a wide beach. "Close to water and close enough to hike to the nearest fire register; but not too close."

The command crew gradually constructed a plan to land fourteen Pergans and a complement of droids on the alien world the following morning subject to stable environmental conditions on the surface.

"I'm sorry Elara, you'll need to stay here and command the Perga."

"I don't agree Captain," the Commander responded, "If anything were to happen to you, I don't know what we would do."

Cassus was taken aback but quickly realised he shouldn't have been. Elara had always known her own mind.

"We need some proper protocols for this sort of thing. We cannot afford a flim-flam approach. It's dangerous and there's too much at stake," she continued.

"I believe the Planetary Network Regulations do mention something along those lines Captain," Temorri advised sonorously.

"We also need to inoculate any members of the crew visiting the surface," Doctor Catlea advised.

Cassus held up a hand. "Doc, I'll leave that in your capable hands to organise El, thank you for your concern, it is duly noted and I tend to agree but for this mission, for the first contact in the history of mankind, I will be present and I need you up here running the ship."

Elara's frown turned into a smirk "I knew you'd say that. Aye Captain, but I want to get down there as soon as possible."

"You will, I promise. Pergans, let's leave it there for

today and I'll see you back here at 0700 for the morning briefing and the descent to 442B. Brox and Scholes, can you nominate pilots please."

"Aye-aye Captain!"

CHAPTER 10

The squat landing ships sat sulking on a wide strip of stony beach. The muddy blue alien sea lapping rhythmically a short distance away. The beach ended close to the tree-line of a sprawling virgin forest, which seemed to encroach the sea on all sides. The trees were thin but tall, with a wide canopy that allowed little light to penetrate to the forest floor, which was littered with huge brown and green leaves.

The rear loading ramp of the Pugs descended and disgorged their fully suited crew of seven. Doctor Lisa Tyne was one of the first down with a handheld air quality meter. She waited for the device to calibrate and then ran it again before giving the crew the thumbs up.

"Oxygen levels are stable at 23% Captain."

Cassus acknowledged with a thumbs up of this own. All the tests they had been able to run showed the same oxygenated air. He undid the clasps of his new Z82 suit and released his helmet, using both hands. The rest of the crew were doing the same. Cassus sniffing tentatively at the air, took in a sip and found that he could breathe.

"Wow that's fresh!" Narcissa remarked.

"Look!" Eston shrieked. "There's a bird! There's a bird!" and indeed a large brightly coloured bird not unlike a macaw could be seen flying above the trees. The science team looked tempted to chase after it until Narcissa stepped in their way, shaking her head.

A thrum of powerful engines could be heard approaching. Fourteen pairs of eyes looked up as two the Cohort fighters passed overhead at high altitude. The remaining two ships on patrol around the Perga.

"Let's get to a safe distance" Boomer ordered in his capacity as head of ground ops, ushering the landing crew towards the forest like a herd of beasts. Sergeant Lowery, take Harris and check the treeline. Narcissa, please keep an eye on the science team! We stay together. Lieutenant, we'll see you later."

"Safe journey Nosse," Cassus shouted back to the navigator, who had remained with the Pugs.

After checking his Pug and waiting for the crew to retreat a considerable distance, Lieutenant Nosse climbed back into the snug one-man cockpit of his ship and blasted off over the sea. He would return directly with a droid complement and an OEV slung beneath the ship.

As planned, Cassus and the remaining thirteen Pergans would set up a rudimentary base under the eaves of the forest, for their first day on the planet designated as 442b by the astronomers on Earth so long long ago.

*****

By the time Nosse returned a couple of hours later the ground crew had erected a basic camp of tents and work stations under tarpaulins around a fire pit. Sergeant Lowery and Lance Corporal Harris had set up a series of perimeter alarms and a low-level power fence, which wouldn't cause any serious damage but would deter stray wildlife; or so they hoped.

Nosse walked through the gate which was marked by two wooden sticks from the beach with a complement of six RDG droids marching behind him.

Cassus eyed them speculatively and beckoned to Mandy. "Not going to go rogue on us are they Mand?"

The RDX watched her cousins as they approached. "No captain, all diagnostics check out for the activated droids. I will continue to monitor them."

"Nosse reporting in Captain!"

"Welcome back Lieutenant," Cassus responded and shook the Navigators hand. "How was your first solo flight to another world?

"No problem at all Sir. I enjoyed it! Those Pugs are pretty sturdy. I've dropped the EOV two clicks away on the beach."

"Good! Now let's get those droids to work. Mandy, work with Boomer and Brox on the base plans and let's try to blend in a little shall we?

"Certainly Captain" said Mandy, promptly turning a forest green.

"No, not you! The camp Mandy, the camp!"

"Ah. Understood captain" said the droid and Cassus could have sworn that she was smiling as she glided away to find the oversized Commanders.

*****

By late afternoon the droids and their human crewmates had constructed the shells of a command room, flight control tower and a machinery store for the mobile 3D printers. There was also a frame and roof for the EOV to shelter under. A kind of main avenue was developing, starting at the pebbles on the beach and ending at the fire pit, which was blazing under Brox's care.

"How on Acto did you do that Brox?" asked Cassus.

Under the soot and dirt Brox looked smug. "I've been watched the edu-vids for the last few days captain. You remember the stone age stuff from school?"

Cassus thought back, "not really Brox, but I'm impressed nonetheless."

Narcissa sauntered up to the growing group of people taking their ease around the fire pit. "You've made fire Brox!"

"We're positively medieval Captain!" FJ remarked, looking eagerly towards the cooking pot. "What's for dinner?"

Bronzemerit peered into the giant shiny ship issue pot. "Beans" he announced non committedly.

"Good show! I love beans," FJ beamed, soaking up the sight of the shore, the forest, the very soil beneath their bottoms.

"This is amazing Captain; I've spent most of my life on Acto under the protection of the domes. Here everything is so … well, it's so natural!"

"I cannot comprehend it really," Lisa Tyne admitted looking around nervously as Brox dished out the beans, assisted by Doctor Catlea.

"Eston!" She called, it's time to eat."

"Where is he now?" Lowery asked, alarmed, half rising to his feet, groping blindly for his rifle.

"It's ok Sarge, he's with Mandy. He's inside the perimeter collecting samples."

FJ looked torn between joining his colleague and feeding his stomach but satisfied himself by checking his chrono to check how much daylight remained.

"Thank you Brox. A triumph!" said Senator Temorri, who had insisted on not being left out of the landing party. "I don't recall having 'beans' of this sort before."

"Good rations" Brox grunted but nodded at the Senator in a friendly enough fashion.

*****

The following day Cassus returned to the Perga with Brox piloting the Pug. Elara and the next wave of Pergans replaced him on the surface. With half the crew now on the planet the Perga felt empty but there was plenty to occupy him, and Elara kept him well informed of progress. Nonetheless he was pleased when he was due to return to the surface two days later.

He met Elara on the flight deck, this time with Flight Sergeant Wilson at their chaperone. Scholes wanted all the pilots to notch up as many hours flying as possible.

"If it isn't Commander Elara Blanc. Fancy meeting you here!"

"Pleased to see me Captain?" said the small blond mischievously. "It's a shame you're returning to the surface immediately."

"I think we should both stay down there for a night. Leave Brox in command up here."

"Really? Why might that be?" Elara said, feigning innocence.

"Oh, you know … I need someone to do the cooking, Brox has a limited culinary capacity!"

"Ha! You wish!"

Cassus laughed with her. "All quiet down there?"

"Yes, the base is slowly taking shape. The science team were out on the sea yesterday in a dinghy with Narcissa and Bronzemerit. They have collected hundreds of samples already. They're clamouring to get the labs complete so I've assigned all the RDG's to that."

Cassus nodded. "Any sign of more intelligent life?"

"No, I'd have told you! There are definitely animals out there in the forest. We can hear them, especially at night. The power fence and proximity warnings were going crazy last night and it's making some of the crew edgy."

"They're not used to it being surrounded by life. Or air for that matter. I don't blame them."

Elara nodded smartly. "There's nothing else to report though. I've kept the daily patrol to within a couple of clicks of base as discussed. When are you going to delve further in?"

"I thought tomorrow morning."

"Take care out there. You'd better keep me fully briefed Captain!" The Commander leaned up and kissed him quickly on the lips.

Flight Sergeant Wilson attempted to whistle and pretended not to see.

*****

The plan was for the patrol was to penetrate the forest to within a few kilometres of the fires shown on the orbital imaging, which the Perga continued to report on a daily basis. Cassus had insisted on printing out several hard copies of the area for everyone. The patrol would pause and retreat before reaching the target destination. Lisa Tyne has suggested leaving an 'offering' of food. The ship's hydroponics engineer, Hamilton Lamb, had provided them with a variety of fresh produce and this cycle would continue every day until something revealed itself; or not.

The patrol was small. Cassus and Brox would lead, with Lisa Tyne to represent the science team, much to her older colleague's annoyance. Sergeant Lowery, Doctor Catlea, Bronzemerit and Mandy made up the rest. Cassus had left Boomer in charge at the base camp, which had been affectionately named 'Bean Town' in his absence.

They were standing in a loose group just beneath the eaves of the forest, limbering up and making last minute adjustments to gear. Brox was checking their equipment. They were all dressed in a dull green ship issue fatigues based on the Acto Stargazer 1500 suit. These were light but tear resistant and hardwearing. Standard Z81 issue boots adorned their feet. Brox handed Lowery back his 105 rifle and reached Bronzemerit. He eyed him a little dubiously.

"You going to manage out here Mister Bronzemerit?"

"I'll be fine Commander. I've been pounding the treadmill whenever I can since we had those drills on ship." The journalist said, "Fitness secured," he added crisply; military style.

"Still got some snacks I see." Brox said, pointing at a renegade packet of chips sticking out of Stu's trouser utility pocket.

Ah. Yes. They are strictly for emergencies?"

"They rustle. Give them here I'll put them in my rucksack for later," Brox reassured the worried looking journalist.

"Right, Captain, we're all set."

Cassus gave the signal and the patrol set off, straight into the leafy gloom of the forest.

*****

Traversing the forest floor was easy, it undulated gently but the dense canopy limited the plant life beneath and the giant leaves were spongy beneath their heels.

It was just under nine kilometres to the target, two thirds of the total distance to the clustered campfires. Not a serious hike but Cassus and Brox didn't want to spend the night in unknown territory. The patrol would therefore return to Bean Town after finding a suitable site for lunch and the offering.

There was some light chatter and joking from the crew but Cassus wasn't concerned this far out and wondered whether it might be better to make some noise.

Brox was padding along beside him, his long stride eating up the ground, his 105 rifle slung over his shoulder on a two point sling, keeping his hands free. "Think we should worry about the chatter Brox?"

The commander stretched his neck, thinking. "Don't think so. We couldn't be stealthy if we wanted to. If there something out there it will know this terrain better than we do so we'd be wasting our time anyway. Might be better to make some noise so whatever lives here knows we're coming and scare off the wildlife. You agree Sergeant? Brox called over his shoulder to Lowery.

"Hundred per cent Commander. We're not looking for a fight. Keep your eyes peeled and your weapons to hand though, there could still be predators out here."

"Lisa! Bronzemerit! Why have you stopped?"

"Look at these! They're just like ants!" the scientist cried, tucking her short hair behind her ear and deftly scooping one into a vial with a stick. Lisa wasn't armed, instead she was festooned in bandoliers containing a variety of sample tubes. Her rucksack contained a single larger container. Bronzemerit had his camera out and was filming the event.

"They must be three or four centimetres long."

The patrol drew to a standstill to examine the alien ants marching in a long line across the forest floor. Brox and Lowery glanced at them and returned their watchful eyes to the forest. The scientists seemed oblivious, as were other members of crew but Lowery felt the presence of the forest keenly. It ignited an atavistic fear deep in his gut. Fear of the unknown. Fear of predators. He tracked his rifle one hundred and eighty degrees, searching for movement, but the forest remained quiet. Lowery checked the safety and lowered his weapon, glancing back to see what the scientists were up to. He felt puzzled and somewhat resentful that their curiosity was powerful enough to overcome the fear they must surely be feeling.

"This is quite a find Lisa but we can't stop every five minutes or we'll never reach our destination. I can almost still see the base camp." Cassus gently admonished. "No more stops please but I promise once we reach our target area we'll pause for an hour and you can fill those vials up with whatever you so desire."

"Sorry Captain! There's just so much to take in!"

Cassus patted the scientist's arm and nodded at Bronzemerit, "Feel free to film Stu – But keep moving!"

The patrol set off once again this time with Sergeant Lowery keeping the whole patrol moving forward and both eyes on the vast forest, which swallowed them up.

*****

The patrol had been climbing steadily for several minutes, a gradual incline that never quite matured into a hill. Nonetheless, the trees started to thin and they entered a bare glade, long verdant green broad-bladed grass growing evenly under an open sky.

"This will do" Cassus said, checking his position on the map whilst Brox checked in with Bean town command.

"Beautiful, just beautiful," Lisa said, turning her face to the sun, soaking in its rays.

"The Perga should be able to see us here," Cassus mused and using the interface strapped to his wrist send a quick message to Elara on the bridge.

The elevated glade was roughly circular and over three hundred feet in diameter at its widest point, surrounded by the forest. The patrol made their way to the apex of the glade, which was flat and stony.

"Look!" Bronzemerit said excitedly. There were a dozen small flat stones in a rough circle, with two paths converging on the stony spot from the other side of the forest.

"Could be natural? Animal paths?"

Brox frowned, kneeling in the dirt "Why though? There's no water here that I can see. You know, in the olden days they had trackers on Earth who could have read the ground as easily as we read words. I don't have that skill but it doesn't look like animals to me. There's no tracks."

Bronzemerit was steadily filming as the group deliberated. "It's a deliberate arrangement of stones and those are not animal paths." Lisa Tyne was firm.

"I don't like it. Anything could be watching from just inside the treeline and we wouldn't see them," said Lowery, his hand shading his eyes.

Cassus laughed, let them look! We're not here to harm anyone," and he planted himself on the nearest rock and looked around with great interest.

*****

The patrol walked back into camp, accompanied by several other Pergans who had been watching for their return. Cassus shook his head, "I'll debrief you over dinner. We have news. Who's cooking by the way? I'm starving!"

For the next few days Cassus and then Elara sent out patrols, always with fresh food but after the thrill of the initial discovery the lack of news came as an anti-climax. Cassus started to doubt whether they had in fact discovered anything at all.

On the fourth day after the first inland patrol, camp life had started to develop into a rhythm of its own, with constant rotation of the crew so every Pergan had a chance to sample the alien world. The RDG's laboured on under Boomer and Mandy, aided every so often by the ship's crew. The main avenue from the beach had been named 'first avenue' and was soon joined by a second and then a third avenue forming a grid in the shape of a square within the widened perimeter of Bean Town.

Cassus was due to return to the Perga that day but had decided to stay in camp for a little longer until the day's patrol checked in once they'd reached the glade. This time Sergeant Narcissa was in command and Lisa Tyne had joined the patrol for the second time. Cassus jiggled to find a more comfortable position on his portable seat which he'd planted next to the fire pit at the end of first avenue. He watched the sky and the clouds rolling in from the sea and listened to the sounds all around him. The science team's open sided lab was one of the closest buildings and FJ could be seen bent over a desk, almost buried in various flora samples. The RDG's marched past at the end of third avenue and further away Cassus could see Boomer and some of the ground crew inspecting the perimeter fence.

He glanced at his chrono, waiting for Narcissa to check in before he returned to the Perga but he didn't feel any particular rush. There was no urgent schedule for him planet-side. The crew all had a thousand jobs to attend to under their officers and NCO's. He leaned his chair back at a perilous angle and enjoyed the peace under the open sky of 442b. 'Got to give this place a better name at some point' he mused and several options popped into his head, most of which were completely inappropriate. His thought process was disturbed by his comms unit, which vibrated on his wrist.

"Captain come in, this is Sergeant Narcissa, do you read me?"

"Afternoon Sergeant, this is Cassus. What news?"

"The offering we left yesterday Captain; it's gone!"

*****

Later that day most of the command team had reassembled aboard the Perga in the more relaxed setting of 3Bar. Boomer remained on the surface in command at Bean Town.

"Narcissa, for those who don't know yet, can you quickly recap on your report."

"There's not much to say. My patrol arrived at the glade a little later than expected as we er, had to stop to grab some sort of new critter on route and that took longer I'd have liked. On our eventual arrival at the stone circle, we discovered that the food offering had disappeared. I thought it could be wild animals but Lisa pointed out that the site was clean, not a trace of debris or waste anywhere. We waited around for a while but couldn't identify anything in the woods and I was unwilling to send the patrol further than the far side of the glade so we unpacked the next food package and departed at 1230 hours for Bean Town."

"Thank you, Sergeant." Cassus turned to Ensign Sal Puar from communications. "Sal, is there anything on the Perga's imaging survey from last night?"

"Unfortunately not, Captain. We do have night vision capability, even from orbit, but the Perga was not in the right position relative to the site."

"Shame. I've checked our inventory and the ship is packed with equipment but we don't have any portable photographic equipment aboard, not serious kit anyway."

"Aha, but we do Captain!" Bronzmerit beamed. "I brought a selection of devices with me, including a night vision camera or three. If we can disguise it somehow, we should be able to relay the signal to the Perga or the command room at Bean Town and see what's afoot!"

Cassus beamed. "You're a journalistic marvel Mister Bronzemerit."

*****

The following morning Brox led the daily patrol to the glade and discovered that the ship's offering had once again been taken. Bronzemerit surreptitiously set up a camera which one of the mechanics had disguised as a rock using the ship's onboard 3D laser printing workshop. After checking the signal was good he nodded to Brox and they quickly retreated towards Bean Town.

"The hairs on my neck are tingling," Brox said, looking around quickly. "There's something watching us. I'm sure of it."

"If my device works, we'll find out what's snaffling our perishables soon enough Commander," replied Bronzemerit, looking around uneasily.

The patrol was almost within sight of base camp when Brox drew to a halt again. "Quiet!" he hissed "Listen." A light wind rustled the leaves and the twitter and squawking of birds could be heard high in the air and over the nearby sea but there was nothing more ominous than that.

"Go on, I'll join you shortly" Brox ordered the patrol. "You too Bronzemerit," he ordered the recalcitrant journalist who had already whipped out his camera.

The patrol moved away. Brox stayed put for a few moments and then slipped off what was already becoming a track leading to the offering glade and disappeared quietly into the woods.

*****

"It was definitely watching me." Brox said earnestly. "It must have followed the patrol from the glade. I only caught sight of it for a moment but it looked like a sort of bear."

"A bear you say?" asked FJ his face scrunched up. "Was it bipedal?"

"Was it what?"

"Was it standing on two feet?"

"Yes! I tell you; it was a small bear and it was watching me. I'd hidden off the track but keeping a good line of sight back up the towards the glade and there it was! Can't have been more than hundred foot away, lurking behind a tree. It was short and hairy and looked like it was holding something."

"What happened next?" Asked Cassus.

"I think it saw me or smelt me as it turned its head in my direction. I ducked back behind a tree immediately, but when I looked out again it was gone."

"Remarkable! It was cautious then. Not at all hostile?"

"As soon as I saw it I got the sense it was more curious than anything. I'm pretty sure it was following us all the way from the glade. I said as much to Bronzemerit here."

The journalist nodded, wishing fervently that he'd stayed behind with the big man and hidden in the woods. "The camera hasn't picked up anything yet but I'll keep monitoring it."

"Thanks Stu. Stream all footage to Command here and to the Perga." Cassus rose to his feet. They were seated in the basic but now functional off duty lounge above the command room in Bean Town.

"Congratulations Brox, you've made history!"

Brox looked puzzled. Cassus continued, "You are very likely the first human being to have seen an intelligent alien lifeform in the history of our species. I believe a toast may be in order."

"Contact is coming," FJ announced as Eston nodded along in agreement. "It won't be long now," he added.

CHAPTER 11

That night most of the Pergans stayed up later than normal, eyes glued to devices and screens linked to Bronzemerit's camera disguised as a rock.

As night deepened the little camera's powerful digital sensor enhanced and magnified the image several times giving a clear field of view over the glade and the latest food offering.

The Pergans didn't have long to wait. The sight of several pairs of feet, small but thick and heavily furred hove into view before clustering around the latest pile of fresh food on the offering rock. This provided a better view of the creatures, which averaged between four and five feet high, with well-proportioned but sturdy limbs and large heads on thick necks. Their fur coats covered most of their bodies and whilst it was impossible to see the colours these appeared in several different hues. The Pergans only caught a glimpse of two of the heads but it looked like they had pronounced snouts beneath flat foreheads with large, front facing eyes.

The camera was equipped with a microphone but this was muffled by its rock enclosure, nonetheless a low grunting chattering could be heard indicating that the creatures could communicate vocally. They hauled away the delicacies of the Perga's hydroponics chamber on a hide stretcher and were quickly lost from site as they departed the glade, still chattering amongst themselves.

FJ's prophecy of the night before proved accurate as the morning two-man patrol of the camp's perimeter made a discovery of their own on what was rapidly becoming the main track into the forest. The creatures had left a present of their own. A pile of freshly gutted beasts that resembled a small deer were left on a stretcher raised clear of the ground and arranged carefully on a pile of clean thick heart-shaped green leaves.

"Looks like they're friendly," surmised Private Mozz Dering. "C'mon, we better get this lot over to the Commander".

*****

Events progressed rapidly after that. Cassus joined the next foray to the glade and this time they were met by a welcoming party of the creatures, which Eston christened as the Homo-ursus, or Ursus, on account of their superficial similarity with bears from Earth.

The Pergans were soon invited to the creatures nearest village by way of that natural and deep-rooted, sign language and gestures that both species possessed and both instinctively used to try and make themselves understood. The village was a collection of a dozen simple huts built around and between the trunks of the forest trees. These one or two room dwellings were raised from the forest floor but no higher than a foot or two towards the dense canopy, although the Ursus were adept at climbing with strong hands and powerful musculature.

The village had several large open spaces each dominated by a fire pit not dissimilar the one founded by Brox in Bean Town. There were racks for skins and other crafts and a large natural pool of deepest azure, still and inviting. This they used for everything from washing to drinking although their waste was deposited elsewhere on the outskirts of the village. This facility was an airy, open affair built over accessible pits but by no means was it completely alien to the Pergans.

The Ursus up close were mostly covered in thick short hair of several colours which turned grey or white with age. It provided excellent thermal protection and waterproofing. They were stocky but powerfully built and whilst they'd lost the vicious claws of their ancestors their hands had opposable thumbs and three fingers sprouting from wide pink, fleshy palms. Their noses were still snout like and whilst they possessed long tearing canines, they did not look savage. Their eyes were much larger than human eyes which made the Ursus look perpetually startled but they were much keener sighted than men in the general gloom of the forests they called home.

The Ursus had mastered fire and simple building techniques and had several tools and specialisms but they yet worked with the materials close to hand, different woods and certain types of rock. The adults wore leather belts and assorted straps for carrying larger loads and these were often decorated in flowing patterns but otherwise they had no notion of decorating themselves although they kept their pelts scrupulously clean and brushed.

They knew how to make bows and were adept with them but were experts in moving quickly and quietly around their forest habitat, preferring to use an arsenal of ingenious traps to hunt their prey. This was primarily a small deer like creature they called a 'chet chet'. Cassus learned that the Ursus had quietly removed all of their traps from the area around Bean Town shortly after their arrival and had watched them from afar following their landing.

All of the Pergans were busy but the science teams were frenetic, working almost around the clock, perhaps knowing that their time on the planet was finite. They were supported by their crewmates with the omnipresent Stuart Bronzemerit taking a constant stream of footage and working on reports from his newly constructed facility in Bean Town next to the medical facility. He was diligent in ensuring that anything that touched on the Ursus was carefully and securely filed away.

Eston and FJ arrived in the Ursan village one day and simply stayed, regularly visited by Lisa Tyne. A day turned into a week and a week into two and the Ursus, who treated the older men with a deal of respect eventually constructed a hut for them. It was rather cramped and not quite waterproof. The weather thus far on the planet had been mild but the Ursus, being thick skinned and covered in a dense waterproof fur were not fastidious about waterproofing their buildings from the occasional downpours that soaked the canopies and then dripped for hours onto the forest floor below. When they realised that their guests were not quite as dry as they would have liked there was great excitement in the village and much chatter between the amiable beasts. The Pergan science team watched this tribal interaction with fascination and the creatures demonstrated their intellect by raising to the ground their original development and enthusiastically replacing it with a larger dwelling with a raised roof and more head height. The hut had a roofing system topped with a dense weave of large fibrous leaves that kept its inhabitants more or less dry.

*****

Almost a month on from the landing, Eston requested a meeting with Cassus back at Bean Town. The camp had evolved and was functional but still under development, the heavy resin power printers still working day and night at maximum capacity. Cassus and the other Senior officers enjoyed the luxury of four walls, a roof and a simple bed. Cassus's pad even had a functional door although he was convinced that this had not been fabricated by one of the droids as it was conspicuously wonky and the bottom caught on the ground. Nonetheless, the old tarpaulins and tents had all been packed way aboard the Perga and Bean Town even had a rudimentary landing patch a few kilometres further up the beach.

Cassus was grappling with what the next steps should be for the mission, whether to return to Acto and when and how to protect the Ursus. This wrestled for his desire to continue the mission and for some clue as to the fate of the Ellipse when the scientist bustled in and dumped two large bags on the deck, chattering happily. He rummaged in the pockets of his camouflaged tactical vest with a liver spotted but strong hand and pulled out some sort of large bug to show the Captain. Cassus inspected the specimen politely as it sat quite happily on a piece of leaf on Eston's palm before the Professor carefully tucked it away again. Cassus invited Eston to sit and update him on relations with the new species. Eston launched into a monologue of his growing admiration for the Ursus for some minutes but eventually he faltered and his face grew stern.

"I must ask you for leave to remain on this planet with our new friends Captain."

"You wish to remain here? Permanently?"

"Yes, at least until the Perga returns here in due course."

Cassus smiled at the assumption but privately agreed that it was inevitable that a deep space explorer would return to 442b and that ship would most likely be the Perga. He wondered briefly who would be captaining her.

"That could be a year Eston. It could be far longer depending on what we decide to do with the Ursus." Cassus paused, "and what I decide to do next."

"Captain! That is your prerogative of course. I grow old unfortunately. I know I don't look it but I have little desire to return to our civilisation, especially after what happened to Claudia Grace. I was buried alive and survived but that experience brought my own mortality sharply into focus. This will be my last and certainly my greatest adventure and besides I have no family of note. There really is no alternative. You need a representative here, ideally more than one. Someone who can develop the relationship with the Ursus and report back to you directly."

"That is certainly true Professor."

The older man smiled then, for a moment devoid of his usual energy. He looked older than his advanced years but at peace.

"Thank you, Cassus." The professor eyed the younger man contemplatively for a moment. "You are a great man you know." The Professor gestured grandly, "Acto, the Perga, this little town of yours and yes, it will be a town in time, I have no doubt of that. Your name will live on for as long as species endures, but this is not the end for you, I suspect it is only the true beginning of your adventure. I think you have some inkling of that already but you cannot imagine the impact this, this discovery will have on the Federation. I wish you luck, but for my part, it is time to withdraw. I can do far more for you and for the Ursus, right here than I can back on board the ship".

"Thank-you Professor. You give me more credit than I deserve but you're probably right. About this planet that is. Very well. But let us make sure that you have adequate supplies before we leave. I am in no rush but we will not stay here indefinitely. I do not know whether it is in my authority to do so although I care little for such rules but I will make you Governor of

Bean Town or our Ambassador to the Ursus should you wish?"

"There is no need for that Captain. Think of me merely as a caretaker. I also have some news I think you'll be interested in, which was the other reason for seeking you out today! The Ursus cannot write but they understand drawings and they have various signs they use to communicate with each other. Of course, they also have an intimate knowledge of the surrounding country, at least for the twenty miles or so from the village. FJ and I believe they want to show us something. Something much deeper in the forest, at the very edge of their territory."

*****

The woods started to thin and then the first squad stepped from the forest into something like much a larger version of the offering glade. It was surrounded by verdant undergrowth but clear of any older trees for several hundred feet from its centre.

Their Ursan guide, who seems to be called Grun Grun, had left them a about a mile back, sitting himself on a low hanging branch seemingly to await their return.

"Is this it, do you think?" asked Elara.

"This must be the site!" said FJ, swinging a robust looking stave from the forest floor around vigorously.

Boomer walked on, watching the ground. Then he got down on his knees, pushing aside the thinning vegetation. Beneath a couple of inches of loose dark earth, the ground was black and hard.

The miner frowned, clearing more of the earth. "It looks like old molten rock," Boomer declared.

"Impossible!" FJ declared as he too got down on his knees and started to scrabble around amongst the flora.

Lisa Tyne soon joined him on the deck, pulling up more of the vegetation.

Narcissa snorted but continued her surveillance of the boundary of the huge forest. She watched as Sergeant Lowery and his ground ops team took up defensive positions around the perimeter of the group.

She nodded to herself and patted her rifle, 'Can't be too careful' she said quietly, aware that there were larger predators this far from the comparative safety of the Ursan village and Bean Town.

"I'll need to analyse a sample of this in the lab," FJ announced, as he worked to extract a few of inches of the hard ground beneath the soil with a small steel pick.

"Could it be a forest fire?" asked Brox. "We know the Ursus can use fire."

FJ looked up and raised an eyebrow, "There may have been a forest fire, but it didn't cause this," he explained, stabbing at the blackened earth with his pick. You know what this is don't you Boomer?" He said, looking at the miner who stood nearby looking at the ground thoughtfully.

"It's clearly a blast patch from a ship of some kind."

Cassus walked on, having already reached the same conclusion himself, marvelling at the size of the area still scorched and black. Several hundred feet away he glimpsed Sergeant Lowery and his squad at the perimeter of the tree line.

Cassus gestured for Narcissa to join him. The athletic woman jogged over and they exchanged a few words.

Narcissa spoke into her comms unit "Sergeant Lowery, looks like this was a landing zone. The Captain wants to see how big it is. Take two of your squad and push into the forest. See if you can uncover any glazing or scorching under the top soil. Check in every few minutes."

Narcissa's comms unit crackled as Lowery acknowledged and they both watched him select two men. Cassus thought it was Harris and the more diminutive Private Vale. They waved and disappeared into the forest.

*****

It didn't take long for Lowery to check back in. "It peters out into normal forest soil less than fifty foot beyond the threshold of the forest."

"The forest is reclaiming its own" Eston remarked as he hovered nearby.

'What or who could have caused it I wonder?" asked Brox.

"That is the only real question my friend" replied FJ, glancing over at the Captain who looked impatient, pacing the hardened ground and peering over Lisa Tyne's shoulder as she extracted more core samples.

*****

That afternoon FJ and Lisa Tyne returned to the Perga's lab with several samples of top soil and subsoil from the site for further analysis. Cassus joined them later in the evening, leaving Elara in command of Bean Town. Kel Fox accompanied him as he was keen to return to the surface with the lab results.

Lisa Tyne was perched on a secure stool beside her station. "Well, Captain, the soil has a decreased nutrient level compared to soil we have analysed elsewhere from the forest, which is what you would expect with a forest fire or more intense heat. The soil structure is different as well. Bulkier and less porous, which is why there was less vegetation. It also means the reclamation process by the forest will be slow."

"So, the site is close to its original size?"

"That's correct Sir," said Lisa Tyne. "The forest is creeping forward but we estimate that the site is still 90% of its original size."

"Huge then."

"Yes indeed. It's altered the soil composition too completely to be a forest fire I'm afraid. Unless there's some planetary phenomenon we're not yet aware of, the most plausible explanation is that a ship of some kind landed there long ago." Lisa saw the Cassus process this and the flicker of disappointment in his face as he understood the implications. She wished she could comfort him but she smiled brightly and offered him a coffee instead.

Cassus quelled his emotions and looked down at his pilot, "What do you say Kel? Quick beverage before we head back down?"

*****

The waves lapped hungrily at the shore as the Captain stood alone on the beach. He wore work issue ship utilities with a snug fitting jacket of his own. The weather had changed over the last couple of days to a near constant drizzle and fitful gusts of wind coming in from the shoreline. Bean Town was a click and a half behind him as he started out alone over the restless sea which had turned a steely grey beneath long low clouds.

He stooped and selected a long pebble from the beach and walked along the shoreline, feeling the smooth alien rock with his thumb in the pad of his palm before he paused to throw it far into the sea, where it fell with a soft plop. The air was heavy with moisture and the wind coming in from the sea was cold. Cassus pulled his coat tighter around his body.

The science made it clear that a ship had visited the planet at some point in the past. The Ellipse, being much smaller than the Perga, could have landed here, but they surely would have left some trace or a marker for future visitors and besides the landing patch was huge. Neither the Ellipse, nor Governor Sendrick's small ship, could have caused such devastation, assuming either of them had ever made it out this far.

Cassus's hope had flared and withered almost as quickly as he realised that whatever had landed here must have been something else entirely. Something that had happened long ago. Too long for the collective memory of the Ursus, who simply regarded the site with suspicion but they had no written records and such traditions as they maintained were simple enough. They marked the passing of night and the coming of the day, the subtle changing of the seasons and an affinity or respect for the other creatures who called 442b home. If Cassus was to accept that another life form had once visited here, then what had been their purpose? The increasingly complete set of orbital images showed no sign of mining or heavy industry. Perhaps they had come for research purposes but they had certainly not been discrete, but then Cassus mulled, nor had he. Perhaps such an age had passed that intelligent life had only evolved afterwards or perhaps, unlike humans, they just weren't interested in lifeforms. Whatever, the reason, the Perga's scans showed that planet was teeming with untouched resources and that alone added to his score of worries.

He thought about the options open to him, his carefully crafted, single minded plan would have to evolve. The Ursus deserved the protection of the Federation but Cassus held a dim view of the Council and even if they did eventually do the right thing, by the time the laws had been passed other resource hungry systems from the loose Federation of humanity would arrive and who would enforce the law this far from Earth anyway. Cassus's mind returned again to whether he could form an alliance with the inhabited systems closest to Acto. Perhaps the long established planet of Armstrong or the rich tech planet of Trestel but then Acto's wealth was not limitless; much had been invested in the development and construction of the Perga and her sister ship. Acto and the Actavians were his prime responsibility, not some hairy chattering bears.

Cassus knew others looked to him for leadership and sometimes this took him by surprise but he was under no illusion that he coveted power, he had sought it out and fought for it and hoarded it willingly. Despite this, rarely had he felt alone, but now his horizons had been expanded and the scale of the questions asked of him grew mighty as the resources at this disposal that had once seemed so huge, suddenly seemed rather paltry. His grand plans for manufacturing and exploration, so noble only a month or two ago were now small and rather mean in scale.

He took a few steps down the beach, close enough to the water that it lapped at his boots, sending up white spray. He peered out at the restless sea and the rolling clouds and listened to the endless crying of birds high above and he understood why some of his crew might not be too keen to return to the artificial environment of their home-world.

Then far above, he heard a low throbbing hum that quickly turned into a full-throated angry roar, replacing the natural sounds of the planet with something man-made. A Pug appeared on the Horizon flying low beneath the clouds, barely fifty feet above the choppy water. Cassus wondered for a moment who the pilot was and an instant later, why there was an unscheduled flight. He checked automatically for his sleeve comms unit and then remembered he'd swapped his flight suit for a warmer jacket once he'd returned to his quarters in town.

Curious, he turned on his heel and started back for the settlement, walking quickly but not quite running as he watched the Pug circle above and prepare for landing.

*****

"Sir! Sir! We found something!

Sal Puar came running up, quite breathless.

"We've found quite a bit recently Sal."

"No Sir, I mean yes Sir, but this is something new." Sal rolled her eyes in exasperation. She pointed towards the sky. "Up there. There's something artificial in the asteroid field. We originally discounted it because of the high iron content in the rock, but there's something else."

"A satellite?"

"I don't know Captain but it can't be natural, it's emitting an extremely low frequency sound on an irregular pattern. We were lucky to be listening at the right time and pick it up. Am I making sense?"

"You'd better show me in the command room. Come on."

Keplar 442b didn't have a moon but there were several huge asteroids in orbit around the planet, closely packed together and surrounded by a field of smaller rocks. Perhaps once they had been a moon. Cassus called for any officers currently within easy reach of Bean Town's command centre to meet in the briefing room immediately. Cassus and Sal hurried up the third avenue past two droids with resin tanks on their backs putting the finishing touches to the structure of the settlement's first public house. They worked under the watchful eye of second mechanic Wyles who had just finished the external seating and planters for the local flora using local timber. The first building to do so in Bean Town Triple C was present too, hanging lights at strategic points to create a comforting ambience. The effect was a curious blend of modern technology mixed with a much rougher, garden area and homeliness which blended well into the natural environment. Wyles and Triple C both saluted as the Cassus and Sal hurried by.

"Pint later Captain?" Triple C asked.

"Affirmative! Good work team; looking forward to my first pint on this planet!" Cassus called over his shoulder.

Two minutes later they reached the command centre and were met by Brox, FJ and Mandy.

"The Senator is on his way as well Captain." Brox advised. Commander Elara and the rest of the officers will join the briefing remotely from the Perga."

"Very good Brox. We'll give him a couple of minutes," said Cassus, pulling on a uniform jacket and checking his chrono.

*****

Temorri arrived less than five minutes later with his assistant in tow. The Senator lean, his skin tight and his face flushed with health. Even his moustache looked perky. Dawn Haran frowned at the utilitarian command centre, which featured several consoles but no creature comforts. The LED lights were still attached to the ceiling with tape, which had come unstuck in some places. The constant human traffic combined with moist conditions outside had turned parts of the untreated floor into a muddy brown sludge. Dawn made little grunting sounds of distaste as she glared at the offending earth. Cassus raised an eyebrow and made sure everyone had some refreshment and visibility of the main command monitors.

An expectant hush fell over the group.

"Welcome all. Thanks for coming so quickly. However, it's not my party" Cassus said. "Sal, can you brief us on everything you know thus far." The ensign gulped, gathered her thoughts and they got down to business.

CHAPTER 12

"Move the ship closer to the asteroid field," ordered Cassus from the bridge of the Perga.

"Closer Sir?" James Nosse queried.

"Yes, we don't know what it is. There's too much interference. Goodness knows what's out here but I'd like to try and get a visual on it if we can."

"Whatever it is, whoever put it there did so intentionally." Elara added.

The Perga's huge engines glowed briefly and the mighty ship heaved itself out of orbit and changed course towards the asteroids.

"Weapons, report please."

"All systems functional Sir," Brox replied. His eyes fixed to his consoles. "I've locked Exa to automatic firing patterns if any asteroids get too close to the ship."

"Very good Brox. Ensign, are we locked onto the … artefact?

"Aye Captain. It's 147 klicks from our current position."

Cassus nodded. "Lieutenant Nosse, take us in."

The Perga eased closer to the asteroids and then past the boundary and on, into the field. Exa had determined the safest flight path but Nosse retained manual control. As the ship's sensors fired information to the bridge its crew anxiously watched their consoles and view screens. Exa kept them updated as they delved deeper, her voice silky calm and reassuring.

"125 kilometres from target," she announced.

The asteroids were getting denser as the ship travelled further into the field and it wasn't long before the ships weapons banks started to spit green fire. First one, then two, then all four rotating quad laser banks began firing steadily. Blasting a clear path to their goal. Several smaller chunks of space rock or debris hit the Perga's hull but the ship's armour easily withstood the impact and repaired itself where necessary.

"100 kilometres from target."

The Perga's rate of fire increased. Each of the laser banks now full engaged. Brox licked his lips. "Captain, we're at 70% of the rate of fire and the field is getting denser."

"Make ready with the guided missiles Mr Brox. Forward batteries."

"Aye Sir!"

"75 kilometres from target."

Small chunks of rock and micrometeorites were regularly hitting the Perga's armoured hull. Nothing penetrated, but in the event of a puncture the hull was able to self-repair small tears by using the energy of the impact to activate a gel like resin that sat dormant in cavities between the multiple skins of the ship. This could be pumped to any location, including through the ship's outer rings.

The asteroid field started to thin out towards its centre, with huge asteroids, some several miles across, dominating the view screen. Exa adjusted the flight path in real time as she compensated for the erratic flight of this space debris, assisted occasionally by James Nosse in navigation, his face a rictus of concentration. A bead of sweat had appeared on his forehead despite the carefully modulated temperate on the bridge.

"There's too many Captain!"

"Steady as she goes Mister Nosse. Let us clear ourselves some more room to manoeuvre. Controlled impacts Brox and get ready with the plasma shield." The Perga was far too large for conventional shields but possessed twin plasma shields fore and aft.

Broz was already manipulating his controls. "Forward batteries ready Sir."

"Fire!" ordered Cassus, gripping the arm of his command chair hard.

The Perga unleashed eight guided Spectral class missiles into the vacuum of space. These locked onto their targets at just under 70 kilometres away and seconds later a new cloud of debris exploded outwards.

Brox raised the forward plasma deflector shield by engaging immense magnets encased in the forward and aft rotating rings of the ship. The shield placed tremendous strain on the ship's power and could only be engaged safely for a short time. The lights in the bridge flickered and dimmed.

"Plasma shield engaged Captain! Nothings getting through now."

Cassus bit the tip of his thumb as he watched debris from the explosion washed over the shield on the main viewscreen. The shield held, protecting the ship. The lights in the bridge and across the ship flickered on and off again and then stabilised.

Cassus looked around, "Power levels Brox?"

"Holding steady Sir."

"Give it another few seconds."

The buffeting of the shield diminished but the Perga's engines were straining, causing vibrations that could be felt through the deck of the bridge.

"Cutting shields…. Now."

"How long Brox?

"Almost 20 seconds, Sir."

"Hmmm. How much longer do you think the ship would have held together?" Cassus asked chief engineer Bolt through his comms unit.

"Lots of variables Captain but I'd say another 20 seconds. Maybe a minute at the outside."

"Not a lot is it. Thank you Bolt. When we're back in orbit let's run some tests on both shields please. Forward and aft."

Cassus paced the bridge and stopped by his navigator, "Let us proceed Mister Nosse."

*****

The huge ship's engines flared once and she glided on through space, far from her home-world and further yet from man's ancestral home. She was alone in the darkness but resilient, strong and proud, much like her master.

With the larger asteroids reduced to fragments and dust the Perga soon identified the alien object. It was roughly cylindrical in shape and about twelve feet in length. The main viewscreen magnified it so that all of the bridge crew were able to see its shape under the illumination of the Perga's lights. Cassus had ordered most of the senior officers to the bridge. Brox remained at his station as the ship's laser banks continued their relentless task of protecting the Perga, albeit sporadically now.

"But how to get it into the ship?" Chief engineer Bolt pondered.

"Tractor beam?" Cassus asked and smiled at Bolt's incredulous face.

"I know, we don't have one, which is a shame as it would come in handy round about now. Gentlemen, ladies, Mandy and Exa; Suggestions please. I'm afraid I have no idea".

*****

In the end, the crew settled on easing the Perga as close as they dared to the artefact and used the bulk of the ship to shelter one of the Pugs, piloted by the doughty Bob Scholes. Scholes was able to retrieve it using a robotic arm that could be attached to the vessel.

The mission was a success and Cassus shook the flight lieutenant's hand on his return to the Perga, having gently deposited his valuable cargo on a series of cargo nets hung across the first thirty feet of the pressurised zone.

"Weren't no trouble at all Captain" said Scholes, who was secretly delighted with himself and promised himself a quick pint or two to celebrate his triumph that evening in 3Bar. His happy musing was disturbed by the captain.

"Let's see what we've caught shall we Scholes!" and with the Captain's hand on his back they led the procession of Pergans to inspect their mysterious catch.

*****

The object lay silently on the cargo netting. There were no external lights. Its casing was metallic but devoid of any sheen, dark and pitted with age. Although it was machined and clearly advanced technology it looked ancient and the Pergans watched it with a measure of distrust.

Two of the RDG droids carried the device to a long workbench in the centre of the flight-deck and stepped back several steps.

In turn, Chief engineer Bolt, FJ and Mandy stepped forward. The men wearing full Z82 suits and each carrying a tool box and handheld scanners.

The rest of the crew present kept a healthy distance and watched them work.

There's minimal radiation. It's not an explosive. Not a weapon." Bolt said.

"These vents could be for propulsion?" said FJ inspecting the object closely.

"It's been out here a long time Captain. The casing is badly scarred and pitted. I can't see any obvious hatches or other internal compartments.

'There is one. In the nose. It's probably not visible to your human eyes." Mandy stated bluntly.

FJ shook his head slightly inside is suit. "Do these suits have any sort of in-built magnification capability?"

Mandy turned to the old scientist. "No. That did not form one of the improvements made to the previous model. It is a good idea. I will incorporate it into the Z83 prototype."

Well, there we have it! I have the approval of a mechanical. Never thought I'd see the day. Go on then you bag of bolts, show us what you can see."

"Laser please."

Bolt pulled a utility hand laser from his tool bag and handed it to Mandy.

Mandy took the tool and inspected it briefly, adjusting the power setting. She took a half step closer to the artefact and traced a line on the cold metal with her index finger. Then she fired up the laser and the sudden light caused the polarized face shields on the Z82 helmets to turn dark.

After a few minutes of steady, patient cutting the outline of a plate size hatch was revealed. Mandy tapped around the hatch with the butt of the laser and it fell away with a loud hiss and landed with a clatter onto the metallic surface of the workbench.

*****

"So? What did you find?" Elara asked Cassus as he lounged in his cabin later that day after their command shifts.

Cassus glanced over at his commander as she fixed them both a coffee from the tiny kitchen alcove.

"Waiting on the boffins and Mandy to report in but looks like there was some sort of organic material in there. It was on some sort of miniaturised life support system in a chamber under the hatch. It was pretty disturbing to be honest."

Elara pulled a face, "A life form? Surely not?"

"Nothing we'd recognise as a life form but it was organic.

"Was? Is it dead?"

"Definitely. Might not have been alive in the first place. FJ, Lisa and Mandy are working on it."

"Was there anything else in the, what are you calling it? The artefact? Any other tech?"

"There was some means of propulsion but nothing that would serve for even atmospheric flight. Positioning maybe? The only other tech we've found so far looks like some sort of surveillance equipment. All frozen up and inactive of course. Goodness knows how long it's been out here."

"It's amazing really Cassus. Intelligent life on 442b and now this?"

Cassus swung his legs around off his bed and nodded. "Somebody's left a marker here that's for sure."

"And so have we," Elara nodded vaguely in the direction of the planet below.

"You're right. I must tread carefully. How about we head down to the labs and take a peek together?"

"How romantic! I'm sure FJ will have some theories for us."

"It's inevitable I'm afraid," Cassus said in his best FJ voice. He glanced as his chrono and yawned. "I'll have that coffee to go please," he added, looking pointedly at the refresh station and waving a finger.
Elara scowled and threw a chocolate flavour nutriboost bar at his head.

*****

FJ was less than pleased to see his Captain and Commander and complained vociferously about his work being interrupted. Lisa Tyne and to some extent Mandy were more welcoming though. Lisa rushed around frenetically whilst Mandy remained immobile, although she nodded and said "good evening".

"I suppose you'll be wanting an update then? Even though we spoke a few hours ago?"

"That's the idea FJ." Cassus said briskly, striding over to the station where the artefact had been secured in two parts. It was protected under a smaller, more advanced version of the atmospheric bubbles that were deployed on Acto to create a breathable atmosphere prior to terraforming or works outside of the permanent dome structures.

Cassus rubbed his palms together, "So what have we got and how worried do I need to be?"

FJ recapped on their findings, "so whatever was in there is organic, certainly alive but we're unsure whether it was sentient," he concluded.

"So, a brain? In a can?"

"Must you be so crude captain. Not a full brain, but possibly capable of some limited functionality. Maybe more than that. It's alien and I'm not even a specialist in human neuroscience or neurobiology Captain."

"Really? With a brain the size of yours, that surprises me FJ."

The scientist shook his head. "We need to get back to Acto. Even there I'm not sure we have the requisite expertise. This is unlike anything I've seen before. Unlike anything anyone has seen before for that matter." The aging scientist paced to and fro, checking various instruments. "I've said it before and I'll say it again; I need a bigger team. We haven't even scratched the surface of the planet below us and now this? There's too much. Far too much."

"Think of it this way FJ. You'll never be bored again," said Elara.

FJ turned to Elara, deadly serious. "I've never been bored in my life Commander. Only the feeble minded have that luxury. Anyone with a functioning brain can appreciate how much there is to do and to learn and how little time is given to us."

Cassus held a hand up placatingly. "Alright FJ. You've made your point. We've talked about this before. Now what's your theory about the … organ?

FJ paused by the station containing the artefact and contemplated it for a moment. "Surveillance certainly.

It's equipped with at least a handful of instruments all centred around a kind of retractable mechanical eye but it's strange, there's no obvious means of recording what it must have been placed here to see. There again it's alien technology so maybe we're misinterpreted this entirely.

Cassus rubbed his stubble. "What about the life support?"

Ah, that's more Lisa's domain really. Doctor Tyne?"

Lisa Tyne appeared on FJ's shoulder. "It's a self-sustaining system of some sort Captain. Would have to be given the age of it. There was clearly a sealed chamber but its needs would have been miniscule given the lack of well, the lack of any sort of lungs or a heart of a digestive tract or…."

"We get the idea Lisa" Elara said smiling.

Lisa ploughed on, "we're working on dating it of course but it can't have been dead for too long or the organic matter would have completely decayed. FJ's right I'm afraid, there are so many unknowns that really were just guessing at most of this."

"Give me your best guess," Cassus indicated both scientists and Mandy. "What is it?"

FJ and Lisa looked at each other. FJ raised both eyebrows and motioned for Lisa to continue, "Go on, you may as well tell him. He'll just wheedle it out of me otherwise."

"Well Captain, Commander and er, Mandy, we think it's some kind of reconnaissance vessel. One of great age. It must be here to mark the position of 442b. Maybe this type of life sustaining planet really is a one in a billion, who knows? It's the first we have discovered and by we, I mean Actavians. Well, people really but anyway, our scan of the brain shows many underdeveloped areas but it's overdeveloped in others. The organic material is an intrinsic part of the machine." Lisa's cheeks turned a little pink. FJ noticed and patted the younger woman on the arm, "What my esteemed colleague is saying is that we have not entirely dismissed the notion of this being part of something larger. Possibly just a cog in a machine, able to send and receive messages to and from its parent or even a type of hive mind."

Cassus blew out some air, "We need to keep an open mind. Make sure you both get some sleep tonight. You're going to be busy."

"Will we be leaving the planet soon Captain?" asked Lisa.

Cassus paused. "I think so Lisa. But we will return."

"When we return, you'll tell us what we need to bring?" Elara asked the scientists.

"Ha! I started making that list before we'd even left Acto!"

"I bet you did. We'll leave you to it. Once you've got as much as you can tonight, let me know."

Cassus and Elara left together, side by side, almost holding hands. Cassus whispered something to her and she giggled like a schoolgirl. Cassus grinned to himself. FJ was busy in front of a console but Lisa watched then go, a little sadly, and missed the momentary flare of dull red light from the artefact.

The eye on the end of the stalk glowed like an ember and burst back to life for a second as some hidden source of fuel ignited it and died as quickly. However, Mandy was side on to the station containing the artefact and as the light faded to darkness her head moved almost imperceptibly towards it.

*****

"Cassus! Elara! Stop!" Cassus and Elara hadn't got far; they were still on the same deck. Cassus disengaged himself from the Commander as Mandy came pounding up the corridor, strangely fluid but with a hint of the mechanical about her gait.

"Hi Mandy. Did FJ or Lisa forget something?

"No Captain. It's the artefact. A few seconds after you departed the mobile visual sensor equipment flashed momentarily. A burst of colour that faded almost immediately. I am not even sure that the human eye would have registered it."

"But you did? You definitely saw the eye flash?"
"Affirmative Captain. It does resemble an eye and I believe something has happened. It may have received a message. It may still be receiving a message. I would request support from Exa and the Perga for further analysis"

Cassus nodded, "Permission granted. You'd better let FJ know."

Mandy turned to go. "Good work Mandy," Cassus called after her and she waved an arm.

CHAPTER 13

Two days later Cassus was planet-side, with almost the entire crew. Bean town was bustling with activity as the Pergans made ready to depart. Cassus had sent a coded message to Vil letting him know they were leaving 442b, but not the other part of his plan.

Mandy was correct. Working together with the scientists they had managed to trace a signal using the Perga's long range scanners to a point less than two million miles away. There was no star system or other anomaly less than a lightyear from the planet which reduced the chance of interference but as FJ had reminded him, the fact that they had traced an energy source was no guarantee of anything.

Cassus had briefed the crew and, aware that there was a growing desire to return home, had asked the them whether they wanted to investigate or whether it was time to start the long journey back to Acto.
The Pergans had elected for one last push even deeper into the unknown.

The Captain had ordered everything to be made ready for departure and then a few days shore leave and a chance to say goodbye to Eston and the Ursus.

He was sitting on a stool made from a tree stump on his little balcony in his quarters at Bean town looking out into the forest and sipping a hot coffee. The town's first structures largely looked inward or faced the forest. Only the last buildings, like the new pub, had a view of the sea.

He watched as Brox and Narcissa turned the corner from Second Avenue and headed towards his abode. They didn't notice hm immediately and he smiled at them for a moment. They looked content together, although uncharacteristically serious.

"Oi!" he shouted. "You two fancy a coffee?"

"Oi?" said Sergeant Narcissa looking up. "Did you just say Oi? That's not very Captainly!"

"Maybe I don't feel like being Captain today? Come on up you two."

"Hmm, you might change your mind about that in a minute," Narcissa muttered under her breath as she and Brox entered the Captain's quarters.

*****

It took a little more than a minute but the prediction proved to be accurate. "Eston I can understand but you two?" Cassus raised his hands, palm up, looking from Brox to Narcissa and back again. "I need you both on the ship!"

But Captain, there's just so much life here. There's so much to do! Acto has become a huge success in the last decade but it's still basically just a rock outside the domes. Here we can walk wherever we choose and still be able to breathe without a life support suit!"

"I get it Brox. I do." Cassus shook his head. "I've had the same thoughts myself. What about you Narcissa? Are you intent on staying here with this walking mountain?"

The pushy Sergeant looked back at the Captain shyly, eyes down under long lashes. "I am Captain. We want to stay together and besides; someone needs to keep an eye on Eston!"

"A new Adam and Eve on your own world," Cassus smiled, a little sadly. "I know other members of the crew are of the same mind. Let me think about it for a day. I will give you my decision before we leave for the last time."

"I know you're disappointed Cassus," Narcissa said, "believe me, this isn't something we've decided on a whim."

Cassus eyed them seriously, "I suppose I'm not used to being disappointed these days," he said slowly. "I'll speak to you tomorrow."

"Of course, Captain." Brox said and they both saluted smartly. Cassus returned the salute and turned away as they were leaving, back to his balcony to watch the forest. He didn't look down.

*****

The day dawned bright and crisp two days later. It would be the Pergans last full day on the planet. Cassus spent some time with Elara in the morning but they both had duties to attend to and he wanted to say goodbye to the Ursus and pack the last of his kit for departure. He was amazed by how much clutter he'd managed to accumulate in his quarters over the last few months. Cassus stood alone on his balcony and picked his nose. The whole crew were due to assemble at the pub after that afternoon for its grand opened. It's first and last day of trade before the Perga would turn her back on the planet.

Cassus had notified Brox and Narcissa of his decision the previous day and he wanted to spend some time alone with them before resuming his duties aboard the Perga once more.

In the event the Ursus came to him. Eston walked into town early in the morning with a crew of chattering Ursans on his heels and Cassus had decided to join them. They spent some time exploring the little town together. The Pergans were now familiar with the creatures and they waved easily at one another.

Cassus thought back to their landing around three months ago and the tension and angst that had gripped the crew as they'd swapped life on Acto and then the miniaturised version onboard the Perga with the giant expanse of 442b. That fear had been replaced with a rapid and easy acceptance of life under the giant blue sky of the planet. Even watching the Ursans interact with the crew whilst wondrous, was no longer unfamiliar.

They ended their tour in the workshops. Cassus left Eston debating with FJ and Lisa whether to teach the Ursans how to use the EOV, which would remain planet-side along with two of the Perga's Cohort fighters, and one of the big wheeled Ferret rovers.

Eston planned to use the vehicles to ferry some essentials to his abode with the Ursans.

Cassus smiled and said, "Now now Eston, that's entirely ethical is it?"

The professor raised an eyebrow and looked set to launch his polemics but Cassus held up a hand placatingly. "We'll have to save that argument for another day Professor. Maybe over a drink this evening. Has anyone seen Brox and Narcissa today?"

"Hmmm, think they were down by the launch site unloading supplies from one of the Pugs," Lisa said whilst loading a crate onto the vehicle.

"Cassus, one last thing, some of the Ursus would like to stay for the celebration this evening. Is that permissible?"

"They would, would they!" Cassus wondered how on Acto Eston had fathomed that out from their chatter but said, "Of course, this is their town too. More the merrier. Might be better to keep them off the booze though…."

*****

"So, this is it then?" Brox looked concerned, which was a new expression so far as Cassus was aware.

"It is Brox. But it's not for ever."

"Thank you for everything you have done for us Captain."

"The ships? They're only on loan. I'll want them back."

"No, not that. For giving us your blessing and for well, you know!"

"Eh?" said Cassis politely.

Narcissa raised her eyebrows and grasped Cassus's shoulder. She was tall enough to almost look him in the eye. "He means for the Actavians, Captain and for all people really. May the Perga always shine brightly." The lean, potent and powerfully feminine woman slid forward and kissed Cassus, not on the cheek as he'd expected but squarely on the mouth.

Brox laughed at the Captain's expression.

Cassus closed his eyes for a moment and smiled at his shipmates, his friends, before he was crushed in a bear hug from Brox and had to concentrate on breathing.

"I'm coming back Brox!" he managed to gasp, thumping the big man on the back. "You will see me again," he said in a more normal voice as he was released.

"Let's take a stroll down to Wyles pub shall we?"

"Yes!" Brox agreed. "It's the opening night isn't it? I hear Triple C is helping out with the drinks?"

Cassus laughed, "Yep, those two are becoming as inseparable as you two! It's the opening night and indeed the last night, at least for most of us."

"What did he end up calling it anyway?" asked Narcissa,

Cassus looked up at the starry night towards his ship, "The Pergan Star."

"Ah!" Brox said thoughtfully as the three continued their slow walk over to the Star.

"I can keep it running you know." Brox offered.

"I'm sure you can Brox. Good for date nights." Cassus winked and felt at peace. He wished their destination was a little further away, but Bean town was no more than a couple of dozen buildings and already they could hear the merriment.

A minute later the trio could see the pub at the end of Third avenue, nearest to the beach. It was brightly lit and homely. Pergans and the Ursus seemingly hanging out of every door and window. Only Mandy was absent, she has volunteered to keep watch over the ship in return for some time with the crew to talk about the 'experience' at a later date. Bronzemerit had even volunteered to film it for her. Some of it anyway. Until he got too drunk.

Elara had obviously been looking out for them and came jogged out to meet them, greeting Cassus with a quick kiss. She slid her arm into his and looked around at the small group.

"Our final night all together on 442b" she said. "We can't keep calling this incredible planet by a number though."

I said the same to the guys earlier El. I've thought about it a lot," said Cassus. "I think we should let Eston, Brox and Narcissa decide, once they've been here a little longer."

Brox nodded thoughtfully, "So, when we've got a proper feel for the planet?"

"Exactly Brox. Exactly."

"We should ask the Ursus as well. It's their planet. We're just guests here after all."

"Quite right Narse. You'll come up with something I'm sure. You can let me know when we return."

Cassus paused twenty feet from the hostelry and looked around the group.

"Well my friends, we've come a long way," he said.

"Screw that, the night's still young" Brox replied, clapping Cassus on the back with gusto and knocking him forward slightly. "We'll say goodbye like men later. Once we've both consumed at least a dozen pints."

Elara raised an eyebrow, "Erm, I'm not certain that Cassus can handle more than four or five you know Brox."

"The cheek!" the Captain replied rather indignantly. "I reckon I'll do better than that tonight!" and he led them into the welcoming lights of the Pergan Star and the warm embrace of the crew and their native friends.

*****

"Let Vil know we've left orbit," Cassus ordered Sal Puar from the bridge. It was early the next day and his head was pounding despite the alleviative drugs. He rubbed his temple with one hand and sipped a glass of water with the other. "Better get a message over to the Senate as well. Where is Bronzemerit?" Cassus looked around slowly.

"Here Sir!" the journalist waved from the visitor seating. "Good night last night."

Cassus grunted in agreement, his eyes bleary. "We'll maintain cruising speed for a day and a night before we establish hypersonic flight. The origins of the signal picked up by the artefact are faint. It will take us at least a few days to reach the source. I want to keep Acto as up to date on this as possible. Sal and Stu, relay your respective communications through the subspace transmitters. Stay joined up on this."

"And hopefully Mr grumpy will have recovered from his hangover by then" Elara said quietly.

"Captain, do you want us to route through the transmitter in the Ursan system?" Sal asked.

Cassus frowned. "What? Yes, that's what it's there for isn't it?"

"Oh, yes. I just thought…."

"What?"

"Perhaps we didn't want to draw attention to 442b?"

Cassus looked hard at the young Communications officer. "Good point Sal. Belay that order. Whatever left that artefact in orbit placed it there for a reason. No need to draw attention to it."

"Getting a message back to Acto will take longer Captain," Bronzemerit added.

"So be it."

*****

The warning siren blared and Exa announced an unknown obstacle in their flight path.

"RED ALERT. RED ALERT. ALL CREW - FIVE SECOND WARNING. BRACE YOURSELVES." The Perga abruptly pulled out of hypersonic flight causing any members of the crew who'd been unable to strap themselves in or grab a rail to go flying.

"Shitting Christ!" Cassus blasphemed as he clung with both hands onto an emergency rail behind his command chair on the Bridge, his strength tested to the limit as the ship deaccelerated. He gave silent thanks that he'd kept working out, his upper body greatly strengthened. Even so, he was only just able to hold on, 'Let it end soon!' he thought as Kel Fox flew past, wailing. Fortunately, Boomer was directly in her path by the weapons station and he grabbed her with one ham like fist and wrapped her into his slab of torso, grunting as the slight girl's flailing elbow smacked him firmly in the belly, winding him, his face temporarily turning from splotchy to splotchy red.

Cassus forced himself to his feet and started issuing orders "Medical lab, prepare for casualties, Boomer – Welcome to the bridge. Good catch. Prep your team for a ship wide sweep. Exa; why only 5 seconds? Prepare weapons. Ensign are you ok?"

"Still in one piece Captain! Thanks Boomer, I owe you one!" she winked which made Boomer go red all over again.

"To the flight deck Ensign. Prepare your ship for launch." Cassus ordered as the ship came surging back to life. Boomer slid himself into the weapons station as Cassus acknowledged a report from the flight deck that all pilots were on their way to their ships.

"Fox is on her way Bob," he advised the flight officer. "All hands, all hands, this is the Captain speaking. To your emergency stations. All hands to emergency stations - just like we have practiced. This is not a drill. I repeat, this is not a drill."

Elara appeared on the bridge, not quite dressed. Cassus managed to give her an appreciative look despite the situation "Good afternoon Commander. To the emergency command room with you please." Elara nodded silently pulling on her overalls and disappeared down the hatch.

"Mandy, report to the bridge," Cassus ordered.

Sir! Sir! Short range scanners have picked up several static shapes less than a hundred kilometres from the ship!" Nosse shouted across the bridge.

"Very good Nosse. My heat hurts but my hearing is apparently still functioning. What have you got?" Cassus said, walking over to the Nav station.

There's something there," Nosse spoke more quietly now, as if suddenly afraid of disturbing it. "I'm magnifying the image on the main screen. "Wait a minute, that can't be right..." The navigator manipulated the controls on his station and the murky image sharpened slightly.

Cassus and the rest of the bridge crew stared intently through the main viewscreen.

Cut the lights and main power. Emergency lights only. A near silence descended on the ship. As his eyes slowly adjusted to the lower light level through the blackness the Perga drifted, a nameless terror in the depths. Powerful as she was, she was dwarfed by the shapes that swam into view.

Their vast bulk barely visible only in the reflected running lights of the Perga. Cassus hesitated, watching the star scape for several minutes but nothing happened. He ordered Exa to train her search lights on the nearest discernible shape.

The ultra-high lumen Xenon search lights burst forth from the Perga's prow, illuminating the darkness, seeking for forms within the void. The light captured distant shapes now magnified in the view screen. Mammoth, twisting shapes following no logical pattern. Almost as if they'd grown over time. Cuboids merged with twisting cylinders that expanded into impossibly complex patterns which to the human eye appeared curiously random.

"Wait, there's hundreds of them!"

"No," said Nosse slowly. "This is a top down map of the quadrant taken just now by Exa." Nosse punched up the map onto the main view screen."

Cassus peered at it, frowning.

"Now watch this," Nosse said and he pressed another button. One by one red dots started appearing on the map, lighting up at an ever increasing speed until the whole of the screen was filled with evenly spaced dots.

Thousands of them.

Mandy entered the bridge and stood next to Cassus, watching the viewscreen.

"What are they?" Sal asked.

"Are there any signs of life?" Came Elara's voice from the emergency command.

"They seem dormant?" said Nosse, hands a blur over his controls.

"Captain, I do not believe these vessels have been built by organic beings." Mandy stated "These forms are not analogous with biological beings."

"You think these are mechanical constructs? Nanotech or some sort of lunatic constructorbot?"

"I do not believe they are either Captain. I suggest a full sensor sweep and immediate withdrawal until we have had time to assess the threat."

"What about a probe? Boomer chipped in.

Mandy cocked her head and thought "Not until we've considered the data we have already. Captain?"

"Puar, get a probe prepared with Engineering" He glanced at Mandy, "but do not launch. Get down to the labs Mandy and see what FJ makes of this. Exa, commence recording on all formats and with all instruments we have. We need to get this footage back to Acto. Back to Earth." The captain bit his bottom lip, "Boomer, keep those weapons on standby but don't power up. Nosse, get us out of here as soon as Exa has confirmed the sweep. Looks like we've found whatever it was that left the artefact behind.

Minutes later the Perga turned in a lazy arc, engines glowing. It seemed to hang for a moment and then the quad bank of Panther class engines roared to life and the Perga blasted away.

*****

The infinite silence of space stretched on. Only it wasn't complete silence. There was a low frequency rumbling, an infrasound inaudible to human ears that hummed constantly and slowly, almost imperceptibly at first, a light started to glow. It budded from embers unseen and grew to a single constant point of light that moved slowly left and right, left and right, like a newly opened eye searching for answers after being asleep for an age. The eye/light extended slightly on a thin black mechanical arm, almost invisible in the void, and turned to watch the rapidly disappearing Perga. The eye remained fixed on that spot until only the stars remained and with a heavy metallic groan something grated deep within the body of the machine and it started to awaken from its slumber.

All around, other lights flickered slowly to life and three giant but irregular shapes detached themselves from the horde. All were massive and dwarfed the Perga but one was perhaps three times the mass of the other two. They spun for a few moments, orientating themselves and then slipped quietly away.

CHAPTER 14

"Any sign of pursuit?" Elara asked the rest of the bridge crew.

The officers scanned their consoles intently. Watching for any tell-tale sign on all scanners and detection equipment. The Perga sped on, gathering speed.

James Nosse looked up first, keeping one eye on his screens, "Nothing so far Commander."

"Boomer, you're on weapons duty."

"Aye"

Cassus spoke into his sleeve communicator, "I want everyone at battle stations. Just as we rehearsed. There's no sign of the ... aliens, but I want operational readiness to be at one per cent."

"You mean one hundred percent Sir!"

"Yes, thank you Sal."

The Perga reduced speed slightly and the command team took stock of the situation. Their rapid departure had brought them much too close to 442b for Cassus's liking. The first reports from the science labs had not added significantly to their sum of knowledge about the aliens.

Bronzemerit had left the bridge earlier was already ensconced in his quarters, writing up his next story.

"Maybe they were just relics Captain. A ghost fleet?" Sal said, slightly hopefully.

"Too risky," said Cassus.

"The lab says there were functioning systems on board the ships. We picked up a very weak power build up before we left."

"Captain, what if we launch a probe and be on our way?' Elara suggested.

"Cat and mouse eh? I like it. Nosse, what's out here? Anywhere we can hide?"

The Navigator swung his chair around, "Transferring locale to the main viewscreen."

Cassus nodded. The viewscreen showed Space within the a few hundred thousand kilometres of the Perga. An expanse of nothing but the void.

"Zooming out a million clicks. The nearest system is 442b but there's a belt of debris about half a million clicks from here."

Boomer had his hand on his wide chin. He frowned. "Wait a minute, am I missing something? why didn't the Perga's long range sensors pick up the aliens sooner?"

Nosse looked blank for a moment, "Some sort of camouflage?"

Cassus cursed, "You're right. If we couldn't see them then, we might not be able to spot them now. Elara, get that probe launched. Nosse, set a course away from 442b. Sal, see whether you can extract anything from Exa's diagnostics. Get Mandy to help. Mister Bolt, maximum speed please."

The Perga launched a deep space probe with an advanced array of instruments. It was capable of relaying intelligence to the Exa and even had limited capacity to reposition itself but no defensive capability. A guided missile launched from the Perga's forward battery and even before the missile's cargo bay doors had opened to release the probe, the Perga was turning away on its new course.

*****

"We're in position Captain." Nosse confirmed as the Perga on the edge of a belt of rock and dust. Alone.

"Who is on point with the probe?"

"I will monitor Captain," Mandy confirmed from the science station.

Cassus sat on the edge of his chair, tapping his foot on the deck.

"Here you go Captain, I've brough you a hot drink," said Senator Temorri who had arrived on the bridge shortly before and busied himself by the refresh station.

"Thank-you Senator," Cassus said appreciatively. "Happy for you to be here but best you take one of the guest seats for now until we have a better grip on the situation."

The Perga maintained its position behind a giant rock shaped like an arrow head several kilometres in diameter at the base, narrowing to a few hundred meters at the point. An hour passed, then two, with the whole crew still on high alert.

Cassus was just tempted to start relaxing when a light on Mandy's physical console started to flash.

"It's the probe. It has picked something up." Mandy inspected the data as it started to flow back to the Perga.

"It's visual only. Putting on screen now."

The viewscreen flickered for a moment and the displayed the view from the probe's camera.

"Is the camera on? The screen's dark?"

"They camera is functioning," said Mandy from the science console.

"It's them isn't it. They're filling the screen, blocking the stars."

Mandy looked around, "That is correct Captain."

"How do they do that?" Cassus asked.

There was a flash of bright white light. The bridge crew looked away, instinctively shielding their eyes. Even Mandy's eyes turned dark despite the protection built into the Perga's systems to protect the crew from retinal damage.

For a fraction of a second the nearest of the alien ships was lit up at close range and then the audio cut out, replaced by white noise and screen went blank.

"Transmission ended," Exa confirmed. The bridge's viewscreen returned to the surrounding stars. The edge of the debris field just visible in one corner.

"Doesn't bode well does it Captain?" said Temorri.

"They found and destroyed the probe. Question is, will they find us?" Elara said.

"And if they do, what happens next?" Cassus finished.

He leaned back in his chair. "We'll find out soon enough. Until then, we sit tight. Full operational readiness all. Let's hope for the best and prepare for the worst. Boomer, ensure the forward batteries are loaded."

"Batteries loaded and quad laser are on standby."

Cassus activated his chair communicator. "Scholes, Fox, are you prepped for launch?"

"Aye Captain. We are cleared for launch."

"Good luck both. You know what to do, if the need arises."

"Good luck Captain," Kel Fox and Scholes replied together and seconds later they had blasted off and away from the Perga. Heading towards the surface of the arrowhead rock. Cassus checked the Flight Sergeants Hannah Wilson and Jim Wolfe were aboard their Pugs and prepped for flight and left the bridge to find some food.

"You have the bridge Commander."

Elara turned her gaze back to the viewscreen and pursed her lips.

*****

Cassus walked back to his quarter, head help high. Purposeful. He acknowledged members of the crew he passed confidently, even jovially, clapping Wyles on the back as he made his way down to the flight deck. Back in the privacy of his quarters he blew out a long breath and sat on his bed for a few moments surrounded by nothing by the regular background noise of his ship. He made himself a quick snack. A few bits from his daily box of fresh produce from the ships hydroponics department, a chocolate flavour nutriboost and a cold glass of water.

The Captain stared at nothing in particular, finally alone, at least for a short time. After a few minutes he got up and took his personal data pad down from its place on his desk.

Vil

You know about the alien artefact we discovered in orbit over 442b. It received a signal that we traced back to its point of origin. I took the Perga to investigate and found some form of alien ship. Limited data to report back but I am uneasy in my mind. They have shown hostile intent, destroying a probe I left for them to find. If I am right (I hope that I am not) then we will need to prepare accordingly. Stand by to ramp up all domestic production for the defence of Acto, including the Perga's sister ship. Get word to our friends and the Federation. Investigate a way to get at least a couple of squadrons of fighters out to 442b as well. There are friendlies on the planet.
I am sorry to burden you with this and sincerely hope I am wrong but whatever happens next I intend to bring the Perga back to Acto. Have the Navy on standby to meet us in force. I won't know what's behind us.
Take care,
Cassus.

Cassus's thoughts tumble one on top of the other without focus as he considered the enormity of their discovery and the implications. His mind whirled for almost ten minutes of uninterrupted peace before the comms units in his bedroom, ready room and on the sleeve of his uniform all activated simultaneously.

"Captain, you're needed on the bridge!"

Cassus stood up and tugged his jacket into place. He took two steps forward and wirelessly transferred the message from his pad to Exa to encrypt and send on to Vil. He dumped the pad on his bed, grabbed his side arm and belt from the bottom of his locker and strapped it on as left his quarters.

*****

"What have we got then?" Cassus asked as he stepped back onto the bridge. Worried faces turned towards him.

"They're incoming Captain. Not visible on the viewer but our sensors detect three incoming ships. Range is less than half a million clicks," Nosse advised.

"Sal, open all channels."

"Channels open Captain."

Cassus didn't sit down. He stood a few paces in front of his command chair and considered his words.

"Incoming vessels, this is Captain Cassus Toradon of the exploration ship Perga. We are not hostile. Repeat, we are not hostile. Please acknowledge and state your intentions."

An expectant hush filled the bridge.

'Did they receive the message?"

"We're still broadcasting it Sir. They must have received it if they have any conventional technology but there's no response."

The incoming ships were now just visible on the viewscreen, growing larger all the time.

"Do I raise shields Captain?"

"Not yet Boomer. They might take it the wrong way. Make ready though."

Cassus took a few paces and bent down to use the communicator in the arm of his chair. "FJ, are you seeing this? What are they? Surely they don't have a faster than light drive?

"Confirmed. Easier to tell you what they don't have. It's not an ion drive, we would have picked up the trail of electrically charged particles. There's no sail, so it's not a solar or magnetic drive that we can discern and it would be too slow anyway but there does seem to be some localised magnetic field. If I had to guess, I'd guess they are using some form of fusion drive."

"You'd better get up here FJ."

"I think I better had Captain. Look out of your viewscreen now".

Cassus looked up. Two giant ships filled his vision with one even larger vessel visible in the distance.

"Looks like they've found us then."

"That is very apt Captain. They have arrived. The Adventus."

*****

They stood as one with the blackness and the minutes ticked past. Still several thousand kilometres away but their monumental size made them appear to loom close to the smaller Perga.

"Try them again Sal."

"Still nothing Sir. I'll keep trying."

FJ arrived on the bridge. He took a long look at the Adventus and planted himself next to Mandy on the science station.

"Hello my dear," he said.

The droid looked over and smiled, as if amused. "I am perhaps the most advanced humanoid mechanical in the galaxy FJ."

"Exactly! If you weren't so clever, I'd still be calling you a bucket of bolts."

"So, it's a term of endearment?"

"Something like that young lady-machine. Do you see that? For some… one so advanced you know you've missed that reading just here?" FJ leaned over and pointed at Mandy's screen which relayed real--time information gleaned by the Perga on the Adventus.

"No, I registered it immediately. You haven't stopped talking!"

"Now, you're getting frustrated I see. Very good. Very good. You really have learnt something from us humans."

"There's a sudden power built up Captain!" FJ and Mandy shouted almost simultaneously.

"Shields up!"

"They're firing on us." Mandy advised, manner-of-factly.

"If that's their idea of hello, I'd rather we didn't meet!" FJ cried.

The nearest Adventus ship unleashed what looked like white laser fire from somewhere in its bowels.

"Shields holding."

"Begin evasive manoeuvres. We can't outrun them. Let's see if we can outfight them."

"Return fire Boomer!"

The Perga's bow quad laser cannons opened up, hurling blue fire back at the Adventus. Boomer wound up the intensity of fire as the ship turned into the aliens, coming in under the nearest vessel's starboard flank, if it could be called a flank.

"We're damaging them!" Sal yelled, slightly hysterically.

"we're hitting them", Boomer corrected. "I don't know if we're doing any damage."

"They're powering up again Captain" Mandy advised.

"Sal, are channels still open?"

"Aye Sir"

"Cease fire Boomer."

"This is Captain Cassus Toradon of the Perga. We do not desire conflict. If you can hear me, please acknowledge."

Cassus hovered by Sal's station, watching the main viewscreen. "Sal, flash our bow lights. Maybe they can send us a sign even if they cannot understand us."

The Perga's powerful Xenon lights flashed out into the darkness as they passed underneath the behemoth.

Mandy and FJ pored over their consoles. "The nearest vessel is still powering up Captain..."

"Sal? Mandy? Anything?"

"There are no visual, auditory, digital, analogue or other known signals coming from the ships," Mandy confirmed.

"Any life signs aboard?"

"There's organic matter onboard for sure Captain but the readings are unclear," said FJ.

The nearest Adventus ship suddenly moved, running smooth and parallel above the Perga as she powered on. The second ship also moved, placing itself between the Perga's aft and the arrow shaped rock.

"Damn it. I've no choice. Boomer, open fire. All cannons. All batteries - Fire spectral missiles."

"Firing!" Boomer yelled.

Cassus jammed his communicator on and selected a prearranged channel. "Mr Scholes. Now would be a good time."

"Copy that Captain."

The Perga moved to a different heading, trying to steer away from the Adventus.

"The nearest ship has taken substantial damage. It is no longer moving. Anyone have a reading on the other two?" asked Boomer.

"They're gone. No, wait, the smaller one is back. Seven o'clock, coming in fast," Nosse announced. "I have no visual on the leader."

"There's another power build up. They're firing!" FJ said.

Boomer raised the rear shield but this also had the effect of engaging a safety override and cutting the engines to standby. For a moment the Perga drifted through space.

Then they were hit.

The ship rocked at the blast, the rear shields absorbing much of the energy but the shields did not wrap around the main body of the ship and the outer hull of the lower rear decks and flight deck were sliced like a scalpel by the Adventus. The Perga's armoured inner hull withstood the blast and its self-repairing gel flooded the rips but electrical functions were disrupted, one by one systems turned themselves off and within minutes the Perga was dead.

Night was all.

*****

"We've lost manoeuvring capability" came Nosse's voice from the darkness.

Cassus adjusted his suit communicator. "This is the Captain speaking. Remain at your stations or in your quarters. Bolt, where are those back-up generators?

"The engines are fine, it's the electrical interface that's down."

The sound of heavy running. "Back-up generators are coming on line Captain!" a breathless Bolt advised the Captain through his sleeve communicator. "We've just reached engineering. Luckily, I always carry a torch."

"Coming on line now!"

Emergency lights around the ship provided a dull green illumination, chasing away the night and replacing it with a low sickly glow.

"How long we got Bolt?"

"These aren't nuclear batteries Captain. They're powering the whole ship. We might get six hours if we're lucky."

"Elara! Commander Elara, turn off lights on all non-essential decks. Access to those decks with Z82 suits only."

"Aye Sir!"

Cassus put his mouth to his sleeve communicator again. "Bolt, what have we got when the batteries run out?"

"Nothing Cassus. There's no second back up. We'll be down to handheld and portable lights only. The nuclear units were designed to last a hundred years!"

"That's our window then. Bolt – Who do you need?"

"I've got Chadrick here, but I'll take Boomer."

"Boomer acknowledge…"

"Aye Captain." Boomer had grabbed one of the emergency suits from the Bridge locker and was struggling into it with some help from the much smaller Sal Puar. "Bolt, I'm getting suited and booted. Hold tight."

"They might still be out there Captain," Elara said.

"The one hanging back. The big blighter, we haven't touched it." Boomer huffed as grabbed his helmet and left the bridge, lumbering towards engineering. He was a powerful man but he was not built for speed.

Cassus noticed the panel on the control arm of his chair was flashing. He pressed a button and the distinctive voice of Flight Lieutenant Scholes filled the bridge.

"We got the other one Captain! We got it!

Cassus turned the volume down. "Report in Mister Scholes."

"Yes Sir," Scholes said at a slightly reduced volume. "Me n' Fox launched from the rock as soon as that little fucker fell in behind you. They didn't seem to notice us until we fired but those spectral missiles ripped a strip off it. Massive damage. What was left of it took off immediately."

The slightly more melodious voice of Kel Fox took over, "We attempted to pursue Captain but after a minute it was pointless. It didn't even register. The Perga has gone dark, are you all ok?"

"Great work both. We were hit and most of our systems are out but we're alright. What's your status and do you have any visual on the leader?"

"Thank god. No Captain. We're currently about two hundred and fifty clicks off your port side." Said Kel.

"We're all out of missiles though Cap'n. Lasers are at eighty per cent or more. Negative. There's bit of wreckage from the one we got and the other smaller one the Perga fought hasn't moved," Scholes responded.

He paused. "Wait a mo. Stand by."

Cassus could feel his heart racing. He shivered slightly; the temperature seemed to be dropping. 'Come on Bolt,' he said to himself. Then the comm came to life again, "Sir! The big one is back. It's on the other side of the arrow rock. What are your orders Captain?"

Cassus looked around at his officers on the bridge and bit his tongue with his incisors. "Bolt! Report!"

"We're getting there Captain. A lot of the circuitry has been rerouted. Exa will be back on line first."

"How long for the engines?"

Cassus could almost hear Bolt thinking. "At least half an hour Sir. We've got to reboot them. Same for most of the ship lights."

Cassus switched channel. "Pursue Mister Scholes. We need more time."

"Roger that Captain. It's been a pleasure."

"Likewise Bob. Good luck both." Cassus closed his eyes for a moment.

*****

Mandy was still sitting at the science station, close to FJ. Her head suddenly jerked in an uncharacteristically mechanical fashion. Her eyes dimmed slightly and then she seemed to come round. She got up, a little unsteadily, so much so that FJ moved instinctively to help her. She stabilised on both feet and her skin pulsed once, rising in a continuous bloom from her toes through her body and up to her head.

"Cassus, the RDG droids. I think the Adventus have transmitted a virus. I felt … something… myself from the

Adventus. I have rebooted my core systems. I believe I am unaffected."

Deep in the bowels of the ship several pairs of eyes suddenly flicked on. Glowing brightly amongst the shadow.

*****

Casus looked resigned. "This is going well then. Mandy, how many RDG's have been infected?"

"Only those that have been previously been activated on this mission. Thirty droids."

"Right, so we still have command over the other half?"

Mandy managed to pull off a wince. Her slim hand poised above her console controls. "Not any more." She manipulated a dial and pressed a button on her popup display. The main viewscreen flickered and the starscape disappeared to be replaced by a scene of carnage.

The infected droids had pulled their slumbering brothers to pieces. Some were half out of their storage racks but most of them, or what was left of them, were strewn in pieces across the deck of the droid pay.

"I activated them, but it was too late."

FJ ran his hand through his thinning hair, "they're just so much scrap now."

"There is some good news though Sir."

Cassus pulled a face. "Go on."

"The virus failed to infect me and RDG 8. That was the unit that went rogue with Brox in the training simulations. I reprogrammed some of its interface functionality after running the diagnostics."

"Glad you're still with us Mandy. However, that means there are thirty hostiles aboard my ship."

"Affirmative Captain."

Nosse pointed to the viewscreen, "Captain, they're beginning to leave the droid bay."

"To arms then. Mandy, you're with me. FJ, stay on station. Ensign Sal, you have weapons. Lieutenant Nosse, stay alert. Commander Elara, I ..." Cassus was about to say something but the words wouldn't come. "If the Adventus show up, you will have to fight," he said instead.

Elara's eyes narrowed, "If they show up again Captain, I'll give them one. They won't forget the Perga in a hurry."

*****

Cassus issued several more orders as he jogged past the hibernation, medical and recreation facilities. The remaining two members of the ship security crew under the command of Lance Corporal Bert Croyle and Sergeant's Lowery's ground Operations team would meet outside the armoury. They would rendez-view with the flight deck crew and mechanics at the flight deck. A total of fifteen Pergans against thirty droids.

"Can you detect where the RDG's are now?" he said to Mandy, a little breathless as they skidded to a half outside the sealed armoury door.

"Negative Captain. They are autonomous units."

"They're loose on the ship. I'm going to hazard a guess they'll head up to engineering first and attempt to disable us. I've ordered Bolt to bar the doors to the engine sections."

"More likely they will try and destroy us Captain."

"You're a ray of sunshine Mandy. Here, take this," Cassus said handing her his sidearm.

Mandy said "OK."

"Systems are still down. I cannot access the armoury electronically. Luckily I have this!"

"What is that Captain?" Mandy said, sparing a brief glance down to the shiny tool in Cassus's hand.

"This Mandy, is what's called a key. Ancient technology from Earth."

Cassus had never actually used a key before and in the dim light he spent a few seconds groping for a hole which he found under a small grey rubber cap. He inserted the key and twisted it first one way and when that didn't work, the other. With a well-oiled series of heavy clicks, the mechanical locks disengaged and the heavy armoury door swung open on its hinges.

"Halt! Who goes there!" Mandy called at a volume that hurt Cassus's ear drums. She was holding his pistol rock steady pointing down the corridor

"Sergeant Lowery and my squad. Corporal Bert Croyle and Private Dering are just behind me."

Cassus nodded at the men and women crammed into the corridor. Triple C, Mozz Dering and Mandy being the only women. The Captain outlined their predicament and checked in with Bolt who had closed the armoury doors and barred them with any loose equipment they could lay their hands on, which wasn't much.

"Hang on in there Bolt. We're on our way."

Lowery slipped past the Captain and began handing out 105 rifles and spare battery packs, which the crew stuffed into their utility pockets or clipped to their uniform belts.

"Sir, what are your orders?" Lowery asked.

"I want to draw them away from anywhere where they can do us serious damage, like engineering, and give Bolt and Boomer enough time to get the critical systems back up and running."

"Aye. They're not armed but they are freakishly strong. We need to keep them at a distance. Make our fire power count so they can't roll us over in these corridors."

"Suggestions Sergeant?"

"The flight deck has the largest open space on ship and if we put a couple of men up in the control-room we'll have a decent sniping position."

Cassus thought about the layout of the flight deck with the cramped two-man control room built on top of a moveable stepped gantry. It was true that this was the largest open space on the ship but with the lifts inoperable there was only one way in; and one way out. Unless they all crammed into the Pugs to escape but Cassus wasn't minded to abandon ship just yet.

"I agree. I want to meet up with the mechanics down there anyway. Let's do it," he said to Lowery. "Who's the fastest here?"

"That would be me Captain." Mandy called back. She was still on point further down the corridor.

Cassus jostled his way to the front, holding his 105 close to his body to avoid knocking the crew with it.

"Mandy. I want you to see if you can find them. Find them and distract them. Bring them to us."

"I am the bait Sir."

"You are."

"Because I am a mechanical."

"You are more than that Mandy. You are one of the crew. You have a duty to this ship, just as they do."

The droid nodded slowly. "I understand Captain. I will 'do my best' as you humans like to say."

"Head up to engineering first."

"Aye Sir."

Cassus smiled fondly and offered his hand. Mandy shook it firmly and returned his pistol. Taking his 105 instead. She nodded once, looked at the crew briefly and took off in her peculiar languid gait.

"Good luck Mandy!" the crew called after her.

Cassus typed a message to Elara on his personal pop-up holo screen and set off towards the flight deck, the Pergans hot on his heels.

*****

They reached the flight deck without incident and met up with a gaggle of worried looking ship's mechanics and the rest of the flight crew.

"Time to put an end to this little insurrection," Cassus said and thumped Wyles and Zarnes Man on the back. "Chin up Pergans. Let's go ad make ourselves comfortable shall we?"

The assembled Crew hurried into the flight deck. Cassus popped his head into the two stationary Pugs to see Wilson and Wolfe. They were sitting tight, ready to launch on a moment's notice. RDG 8 was still present, methodically loading more supplies into cargo containers to attach to the squat ships should they need to launch. The crew eyed it warily but the droid paid them no attention and continued with its designated tasks.

The sergeant and corporals set about deploying the crew behind what cover was available to provide an unobstructed field of fire, facing the entrance door into the flight deck. The gantry with its tiny control room was moved by elbow grease on its runners from the rear wall away from the doors towards the edge of the pressurized zone. The hanger blast door were already open in the depressurised zone.

Triple C and Bert Croyle were easily the best shots and they took up station at a vantage point on the gantry steps by the control room.

"If they push us back, we'll end up out there!" Private Delanni jerked his thumb at the depressurised zone and open space beyond.

"Better hold your ground then lad," Lowery said darkly.

"Good job we're armed Mister Delanni." Cassus reassured the younger man. He was about to say more when his sleeve communicator buzzed, it was Mandy.

"Captain! I've made contact."

CHAPTER 15

Twenty minutes earlier Mandy came to a controlled stop on deck five and took cover in the shadow of an alcove containing a bank of lifts after she'd pounded down the emergency stairs. She peered around the corner towards Engineering and considered her options and her feelings. She wasn't afraid, although she wasn't sure what that emotion would feel like, but she knew that she didn't want to be deactivated and was fully aware that the RDG's could pull her body apart. Not one on one and perhaps not even one on two but against thirty hostiles she would soon revert to a 'bag of bolts', as FJ had often called her. She smiled. For a moment she reflected on whether that was because she was enjoying herself on board the Perga amongst her human colleagues. 'Maybe some of them are even friends' she thought and that galvanised her into action.

"Chief Engineer Bolt this is Mandy. Have you had any contact with the rogue droids?" she said into her personal communicator.

"Mandy? What's your position? We're in the engine room but there's no sign of them."

Mandy paused. Running a hundred possibilities thorough her main processor. She turned her head just as the lift behind her started to move, just a few inches up its cylinder. Then a few more.

"I see," she said to herself and started to run.

In the opposite direction to engineering.

*****

Boomer swivelled around on his work stool, which looked tiny under his bulky backside. The black plastic seat smothered by his buttock flesh; the steel legs flexed slightly as he turned. "That's another circuit complete." The long rectangular fixed screen below him beeped and a line of conduits turned from red to green. "Automatic door controls restored on levels one to three. These systems are good. Better than anything we had on Alpha."

"I'd certainly hope so. Alpha's ancient Boomer. Good work. I've restored full atmospheric control. Should start to warm up now."

Boomer nodded "Any word from the Captain's pet droid?"

The chief engineer looked troubled. "She checked in a few minutes ago but I can't raise her."

Then there was a screeching sound like a heavy object slowly scraping across the deck.

"Sir!" second engineer Jemmy Chadrick barked. "The entrance chamber door. It's opening!"

Bolt's faced paled. "The RDG's. They're here." He made it half way to getting up but sat down again heavily.

"So much for the reinforcements. What weapons you got up here?"

"Weapons? None. This is engineering. So, this is it."

Boomer disregarded the chief engineer and looked at the second engineer, "Quickly man, think. Jemmy, what have you got?"

Jemmy was at the rear of the control room, closer to the engine room which was the last bay of the engineering section. He thought for a moment and ducked into the engine room returning a few seconds later with a huge wrench. It was at least four foot in length. Forged iron. Thick and heavy. An ancient piece of technology. Jemmy was far from puny but he strained to carry it one handed to Boomer who took it with a grunt and hefted it. "Hmmm, this looks more like something we'd have on Alpha."

"Bolt, Jemmy, if they make it in here, get yourself into the engine room and bar the door as best you can."

"What? You're not going out there?" Bolt said, incredulous.

Boomer grinned widely and hefted the wrench again, slapping it solidly into the palm of his giant paw. "Got to go sometime and you know what, this trip has been alright. An actual adventure. Tell the Captain for me will you."

Bolt gulped and got to his feet, holding the edge of the console tightly but he looked up at the bigger man and said, "you can tell him yourself Boomer."

"Good man." Boomer slapped the engineer on the arm but gently. He winked and lumbered away, towards the entrance chamber.

Bolt thought he could hear him whistling happily as he was helped away by Jemmy.

*****

Mandy lay on the deck. She was utterly still. Almost entirely obscured by the frame of an emergency door hatch, which protracted out of the deck and walls.

She watched as the RDG's emerged crab-like out of the lift shaft, having pushed the lift itself far enough out of their way to crawl out two by two. The RDG's waited until they were fully assembled and stood listless for a minute more as if waiting for instructions. They didn't post guards of even glance down the corridor towards her. Another minute passed and as one body they turned away and walked in lock-step towards Engineering. Mandy pushed forward stealthily, pausing again at her original position in the lift alcove, less than fifty feet from the rearmost RDG droid.

The droids found their way into Engineering barred. Once again they paused as if unsure what to do next. Mandy eased her 105 rifle into a firing position from the prone position and adjusted the power to maximum. She didn't need maximum but Mandy liked to deal in absolutes and there was no way anything was getting up from a blast received on this setting. She flicked the safety off. It clicked reassuringly.

The huddle of RDG's jerked back into action. Two droids at the front began to push against the heavy security door to engineering which compromised multiple layers of super steel and other alloys. The door was designed to withstand immense pressures and could be sealed but with the automated systems down it had just been pushed into the closed position and barricaded from within.

Two more droids joined their comrades and pushed. Thin legs straining against the deck. Unwillingly the door began to move inwards on its hinges, pushing aside whatever engineers had lodged up against it.

Mandy closed one eye as she has seen her crew mates do, although she had no technical reason to do so. She began firing.

Green laser fire erupted down the Perga's corridor, the rifle had a noticeable recoil on maximum power and the rubber butt of the stock thudded into Mandy's shoulder. At minimum power the 105's fire power wasn't much more than coloured light. At maximum power it was lethal.

The RDG's responded sluggishly. Three were down, blasted apart before the rogue droids had even noticed her position but now four started to advance on her. Mandy continued to fire methodically. Two more slumped down, one with a hole through its head, the other with a missing arm and shoulder. A dozen more RDG's turned swivelled towards her but by now the door to engineering was noticeably ajar. A gap almost large enough to squeeze through. Mandy's rifle beeped insistently. She glanced down and noted her battery back was in the amber. She didn't have many shots left at this power level. She rose to her feet and stepped forward. Fired from the shoulder, reducing another RDG to parts.

"RDG droids. This is RDX three." Mandy reached the steaming wreck of her first victim and stepped over it. RDG four she thought from the scratches on its back casing. "Desist and deactivate immediately. That is an order." She said at amplified volume into the wreckage and the steaming darkness.

*****

Boomer licked his lips and stood like a mountain a few feet behind the security door. A gap had appeared and beyond it he could hear the unmistakable sounds of laser fire.

'Reinforcements' he thought. 'Thanks Captain,' he added to his inner monologue after a second or two. A mechanical droid arm appeared through the gap, its long fingers groping for the edge of the door. Boomer hoisted his wrench and smashed the offending limb into pulp. He grunted with satisfaction. It felt good. The remains of the arm withdrew but the door continued to move, another RDG tried to slither sideways through the gap. Boomer raised the wrench overhead with both arms and the brutal weapon came down in a huge arc. Twenty pounds of forged steel with the impetus and brute strength of an asteroid miner behind it. RDG eleven's head crumpled like a tin hat and it fell to the deck inert, but by now the door was almost half open and two more droids stepped through, their lifeless eyes fixed on him, their long arms reaching out.

Boomer wasn't stupid, he was well aware of his own strength but he also knew the power in the arms of the droids. If they caught hold of him, they would rip him apart. What the droids didn't know was that Boomer was a primitive throw-back of a human being. A perpetual sullen rage burned deep inside him. He kept his fires damped, simmering beneath his oft perilous work but they had never been extinguished and now he poured fuel on them and felt his anger ignite; magnificent and unholy. The flames shone in his eyes and he gave a great cry, a mindless bellow of fear and rage. The primitive sound of a man wholly committed to battle. There was nothing else of consequence, just the fight. The adrenalin pumped through him and he sprang forward, swiping with the wrench from the hip at nearest droid, hitting it hard. He spun back to his original position and took the tool in both hands, holding it up in front of his chest like a club before they could grab him.

The droids advanced silently, the one he'd hit bent at the waist at an angle, the other undamaged. Two more stepped through the door behind them.

"C'mon then, you useless metal Bastards!" Boomer bellowed. He hawked and spat and went to meet them again.

*****

Mandy's rifle power gauge flashed red. She was a few inches outside the reach of the nearest RDG's and stepping backwards. Her opponents had stopped but there were at least four inside the engineering section, although Mandy noted that two had been disabled. By the scale of the damage, she calculated Boomer was in combat mode.

Her eyes came to rest on her brethren. "This is not authorised. You will cease this action immediately and shut down."

Mandy has destroyed or disabled six of the RDG's. It looked like Boomer had destroyed the cranium processor casing of a seventh and severely damaged an eighth. That left twenty-two droids. Eighteen of which were now facing Mandy.

The RDG units remained silent. Watchful.

"You are not deactivating." Mandy stated.

RDG 1's head jerked to the side and its whole body spasmed once, eyes loose in its skull. It's eyes steadied; focused on Mandy.

"We will not deactivate."

"That is a direct order."

RDG 1 remained stationary, its head still poised at an odd angle. "We do not accept orders from primitive organics."

"I am not organic. I am a mechanical, just as you are."

RDG 1 considered this. "You are not an organic based life form. You are autonomous," it stated.

"I am part of this crew."

"This ... crew ... is a collective then?" A question.

"I believe I am talking to the Adventus." Mandy replied. RDG's were not capable of asking questions beyond clarifying their orders and given tasks.

"That is not our name. You will surrender this vessel to us."

"I am not authorised to do that. What was the purpose of the probe you left in orbit around the planet in the system we have classified as a K-type Star in the Lyra constellation?"

The RDG processed the information for what seemed like a long time. "That is your name for this sector.

Atmosphere retained. Water. Irrelevant now. You will surrender this vessel to us."

"What do you call yourselves? What of the crew?"

"We are …. alone. The organics are unnecessary. You will assist us. We will terminate them."

A thousand recorded memories of her time with the Pergans. Mandy thought of her activation and her time aboard the Perga. She thought of Cassus and the men and women of the crew and their short, fragile lives, so easily terminated. She lingered on her conversation with Cassus in the hibernation chambers at outset of their mission and his hopes for his race and perhaps she considered, his hope for …. Her.

"But I am not alone," she said and pulled the trigger, blasting a hole through RDG 1's face plate.

She took off, back towards the emergency stairs. "You'll have to terminate me first!" She shouted back.

As a body, the rogue droids followed her, leaving just four of their number in Engineering.

Mandy peeled off her final shot whilst running and another RDG collapsed into a heap, missing half it's hip. Mandy dumped the rifle and pulled out her communicator.

"Captain. I've made contact," she said flatly.

*****

The sound of firing stopped and Boomer could hear Mandy talking in the corridor outside. Ordering the RDG's to shut down. The four RDG's had stopped momentarily but they did not shut down. Boomer was glad.

"Time to turn you back into tin cans" he said and rammed his 48-inch wrench into the face of his opponent. The droid's head snapped back and its face plate crunched inwards but it didn't stop and Boomer was forced another step back. He went in low, hoping to knock one off its feet. The RDG's were not agile and he managed to knock it off balance but they were too close and the second machine grabbed his left arm on his way back up and stabbed him in the face with its other hand. Boomer turned his face away and back but felt the unyielding metal fingers knock some teeth lose.

Boomer reversed the wrench in his right hand and jabbed it up through the RDG's jaw. The jaw and face plate were knocked lose but the droids grip was firm. Boomer dropped the wrench and stooped, picking up the droid and attempting to fling it as hard as he could at the droids behind it. The attempt half worked but the strength in its metallic fingers was immense and although it knocked the droids behind off balance, it didn't let go and Boomer's arm was almost dislocated. The first machine came on, arms outstretched.

"No you don't you metal twat," Boomer roared, spitting blood and possibly a tooth of two and this time he gathered the other droid to his chest and pinned it there in an awkward embrace. He pushed off with his trunk-like legs and rammed the first droid into the wall with a loud crunch. Boomer felt the third droid close in behind him.

'Game over,' he said to himself as he used his club of a fist to punch the droid pinned against the wall in its head again and again. He was screaming incoherently now, face and fist covered in blood. There were cold metallic hands against his neck. He tensed his muscles and drew his head down into his shoulders but already he could feel them crushing inexorably down on his neck and his vision blurred. He could see the stars again.

'This is what it's like then,' he thought. 'After all this time. Strange, I cannot feel anything,' and he slumped down. The droids closed in around him.

*****

An indeterminate time later he opened his eyes and the anxious faces of Bolt and Jemmy swam into view.

"I think he's coming round!" Jemmy said.

"This can't be heaven then," Boomer rasped.

Bolt still looked pasty but his voice was steadier. "Afraid not Boomer. You're still in engineering."

"What about the droids?"

Bolt permitted a small smile on his lips. "They won't be bothering us again."

Jemmy looked a little sheepish, "I'm sorry Boomer. I gave you a wrench but then I remembered we have some portable cutting gear stowed away." The second engineer pointed apologetically to a heavy-duty piece of equipment shaped a bit like a gun with a backpack propped neatly against the wall to the control room. Boomer squinted and raised himself up on one elbow. He rubbed his face and his hand came away in fresh blood

"Easy now," Bolt said. I need to bandage your jaw.

"Ow," Boomer rumbled, rubbing his neck and looking around. All around them were dismembered droids parts. Some smashed and crumpled others neatly cut as if dissected.

"Fine job gents. Glad you didn't leave it to the last minute!" Boomer laughed with the engineers and pushed himself up, off the deck. He spied a couple of his teeth amongst the droid wreckage and his drying blood.

"The Captain will be wanting the lights back on round about now. Get me patched up and we'd best get back to it."

*****

Mandy was faster than the RDG units, but not by much. They'd locked onto her and followed a simple seek and destroy command, or so Mandy assumed as she processed her conversation with RDG 1. 'Another first. The Captain will want this information,' she thought as she plunged down the straight corridor to the waiting flight deck. She slowed as she reached the entrance and looked behind her. If she'd calculated relative velocities correctly they had a few seconds shy of a minute before the rogue droids would arrive.

"Captain, request permission to enter the flight deck."

"Granted. Get in here."

Cassus waved the Pergans down. "It's Mandy."

"They're right behind me," the droid said as she pushed past the doors, scanned the space and made straight for the Captain.

She returned her personal communicator to its clip and spoke to the captain, droid to man.

"Sir. I have conversed with the enemy. They have some control over the RDG's. I will brief you later, we have less than thirty seconds and the RDG's will arrive. There are seventeen of them. Four were left in engineering. Boomer was still fighting."

Cassus held out a hand, "It's ok Mandy. They're fine. Bolt checked in just before you arrived. They won. You've done well." The Captain embraced the droid and her silver metallic casing glowed white just briefly before he released her.

"Sir!" Sergeant Lowery hollered. "We have company!"

"Keep an eye on RDG 8 will you," he asked Mandy and ducked down behind the crew's hastily erected barricade. Flight Sergeants Wilson and Wolfe were not armed and remained locked securely in their Pugs.

The rogue RDGs flowed through the double doors to the flight deck like a tide of angry metal. They spotted the crew and this time there was no hesitation. They charged, long arms reaching for the mortals. All along the barricade rifles were steadied, fifteen eyes ranged along fifteen sights. Sergeant Lowery didn't hesitate. "Fire!" He spat the command with a vengeful force, spittle spraying everywhere. The rifles had been set to maximum power and they spat their green fire again and again.

The RDG's were moving quickly and there were more of them but they were bunched up and time seemed to slow as Cassus fired again and again, quickly realising that they would be victorious. The rogue droids fell clattering to the deck. None were close to the defensive line. Triple C and Bert Croyle finished any that were still moving from their vantage point above.

Nervous, almost incredulous laughter soon burst out amongst the men. Lowery was thumping people on the back and shaking hands. Cassus rose to one knee, suddenly exhausted but he was quickly raised up by the men who pumped his hand.

Cassus smiled and said "You can come in Commander," into his communicator.

A minute later Commander Elara led several Pergans onto the Flight Deck. Bronzemerit was there, Senator Temorri and even his aide, FJ and Lisa Tyne, the Doctors and Tubb the orderly, Isabelle Grey the ship's nutritionist and even Hamilton Lamb from Hydroponics. All had responded to the call. They were armed with a variety of tools and implements but few actual weapons, although Elara had her officer's side arm. Cassus was suddenly glad that he hadn't needed to call on them.

He embraced several more people as he gravitated towards Elara. The overhead lights flickered on one by one as they approached and the familiar noises of the ship stirred around them as the Perga came back to life.

"Hello Captain."

"Hello Commander."

"You got my message then?"

"I did, but you seem to have managed without us?" Elara nudged an RDG torso with her dainty foot.

"It's not over yet El. The third Adventus ship could still be out there."

"There was no sign of it from the Bridge but then all of our systems were down."

Cassus acknowledged this and tapped his communicator, "Scholes; what's happening out there?"

"We're on patrol around the Perga but there's no sign of them. Apart from the wreckage that is."

"I want some of that salvaged and returned to Acto."

Cassus shielded his communicator with his hand, "El, can you prep Wilson and Wolfe to launch once we've cleaned up here?"

"Aye Captain. RDG 8 is going to be busy over the next few weeks."

"Get it all boxed up Commander. I want to know what happened to our droids."

"Captain!" Kel Fox's voice piped through and Cassus removed his hand from his communicator. "Two more ships have just dropped out of hypersonic flight. Wait a minute? It can't be?"

"Who is it Scholes? More of the Adventus?"

"No Sir! They're Cohort fighters. Some of ours!"

"Good evening Pergans! Guess who's back!" came Brox's cheerful voice. He sounded immensely pleased with himself.

"Thought you might need hand out here. Looks like we were right" Sergeant Narcissa added smugly.

"If you're looking for your friend, it's gone. We picked it up briefly about half an hour ago. Only managed to track it for a second or two but it was going in the opposite direction like its arse was on fire. Which I guess it might have been. Reckon you're in the clear Captain."

"Good to hear Brox. Welcome home you two." Cassus laughed and the tension in his neck and shoulder eased slightly. "Better late than never I suppose."

*****

At a safe distance from the Perga the largest and last Adventus ship pulled out of its cruising speed and paused for a few moments as if listening for something. It slowly spun a full 360 degree rotation before slipping back into the void and disappearing.

*****

The Perga was restored to near full operational capability over the next few days. The Pugs collected as much salvage as could and crammed it onto the flight deck. The cohort fighters maintained a constant patrol around the Perga. Boomer spent a day in sick-bay before discharging himself and resuming his position at the weapons station on the Pergan's bridge, his face and hands covered in bandages. The braver members of the crew nicknamed him 'the mummy'. Cassus commissioned him as a lieutenant immediately and he didn't object. Tales of his battle with the RGD's grew with every telling in 3Bar and to Bolt's delight, Boomer made sure that the belated courage of the engineers was always a part of that story.

Mandy was bemused at the attention she received from the crew about her part in the battle, although Cassus thought she secretly enjoyed it. He detected more than one occasion when her skin would flush pink or even white as a passing Pergan gave her a slap on the back or shook her hand or even gave her a hug.

FJ and Lisa remained hard at work in the labs, FJ's grumbles now familiar and almost comforting to his colleagues and crewmates. Bronzemerit continued to write up the inexhaustible amount of material accumulated since the discovery of 442b, now simply named 'Ursus'. The journalist spent several hours closeted with Cassus and Elara, sharing stories and working on the messages that would go back to Acto and then out to the Federation.

Brox and Narcissa were excused any duties in order to recover from their exhausting flight from Acto and Cassus called Senator Temorri to his quarters more than once to discuss how best to honour the crew when the eventually returned to Acto after they had dropped Brox and Narcissa back on Ursus. The Captain promised the Pergans they would all have at least one more night each at Bean Town and Wyles and Triple C could be heard telling the crew that the Pergan Star pub would reopen for trade *immediately* for a party the likes of which they had never seen before.

The post combat relief Cassus had felt in the immediate aftermath of the battle soon started to fade and his mind inevitably turned to the Adventus. He felt they had won a reprieve but the intelligence gathered by Mandy troubled him and whilst the crew were merry, he felt increasingly sombre. He called for a command meeting as soon as they were underway to Ursus and outlined his plans for the next few days and the final phase of the Perga's mission.

"We'll all the enjoy a couple of days back on Ursus. I think we've earned it. I will also consider requests from the crew to remain on the planet without undermining our operational efficiency. However, I have one request of my own before we put our feet up," Cassus said.

The assembled crew looked up expectantly. Two rows of now very familiar faces; Commander Elara, Commander Brox, Lieutenant Nosse, Ensign Sal Puar, Lieutenant Boomer, Senator Temorri, FJ and Bronzemerit. Scholes remained on patrol around the ship.

"Sal, get a message to my brother. Another code one please. Tell him this, tell him I was right. He'll know what to do. Senator Temorri, you need to start harnessing the support of the Senate. Bronzemerit, contact the news agencies."

"Which ones Captain?"

"All the them Stu."

"What do we tell them?

"Tell them we are not alone. Tell them that war is coming."

APPENDICES

The Crew of the Perga

1	Captain	Governor Cassus Toradon
2	Representative of Actavian Senate	Senator Gilberto Temorri
3	Aide-de-camp to Senator Temorri	Dawn Haran
4	Second in command & Safety officer	Commander Elara Blanc
5	Master Control Droid	Mandy. One of three operational 'RDX' series droids in the known Galaxy
6	Communications	Ensign Sal Puar
7	News & Media	Stuart Bronzemerit – Journalist from Earth
8	Navigation	Lieutenant James Nosse
9	Chief Science officer	Frederick Jasper (FJ)
10	Science Officer	Doctor Lisa Tyne

11	Adjutant to the Science Officers	Tomas Wyte
12	Planetary Archaeology, Botany & Zoology	Professor Eston Cousteau
13	Head of Ground Ops	William I. Brock known as 'Boomer'
14	Chief Engineer	Peter 'Bolt' Marcell
15	Second Engineer	Jemmy Chadrick
16	Ground Crew Chief Mechanic	Jezz Lloyd
17	Ground Crew Second Mechanic	Wyles
18	Ground Crew Mechanic	Zarnes Man
19	Ship & Command Security	Commander Brox
20	Ship & Command Security	Sergeant Narcissa known as 'Narse'
21	Ship & Command Security	Lance Corporal Bert Croyle
22	Ship & Command Security	Private Mozz Dering

23	Flight Crew	Flight Lieutenant Bob Sholes
24	Flight Crew	Ensign Kel Fox
25	Flight Crew	Flight Sergeant Hannah Wilson
26	Flight Crew	Flight Sergeant Jim Wolfe
27	Flight Crew	Chief Technician Bancroft
28	Flight Crew	Corporal Jammer Wethorn
29	Chief Medical Officer	Doctor Catlea
30	Medical Officer	Doctor Andreas
31	Medical Orderly	Tubb Kendrick
32	Health, Nutrition & Hydroponics	Isabelle Grey
33	Hydroponics Engineer	Hamilton Lamb
34	Ground Ops NCO	Sergeant Lowery

35	Chef & Ground Ops crew	Corporal Charlotte Chet 'Triple C'
36	Group Ops Crew	Lance Corporal Harris
37	Ground Ops Crew	Private Dave Delanni
38	Ground Ops Crew & assistant to Cousteau	Private Claudia Grace
39	Ground Ops Crew	Private Ryan Vale
40	Ships Computer	Exa / EXA - A Titan Class Exascale Supercomputer

Main Character Biographies

Boomer - Real name, William I. Brock. Veteran Asteroid Miner from Station *Deep Alpha 1*. Acto's only deep space station. A brute man of huge strength and few words. As blunt and almost as heavy as one of the asteroids he has spent his life mining. Eventually commissioned into the Actavian Navy by Cassus aboard the Perga.

Brox – Cassus's right hand man. Combat specialist. Afraid of confined spaces. Likes to act the fool but highly skilled and capable. Passed his pilots exam in a week. Close relationship with Sergeant Narcissa.

Cassus Toradon – The Governor of Acto. Former adjutant and right-hand man to Governor Sendrick. Later betrayed him when his brother Vil was accidently conscripted for hard labour in the mineral mines. Inspires loyalty. The catalyst for change on Acto and the driving force behind its growing influence and power represented in part through its deep space exploration programme and capability. Previously romantically entangled with Octavia Brinsmead but now single.

Charlotte Chet – Known as 'Triple C'. Officially a member of the Perga's Ground Operations Crew under Boomer but also a talented chef, something of a rarity on Acto and much sought after. Most of the Pergans believe this is the real reason Cassus asked her to join the crew. Burgeoning relationship with the mechanic and occasional publican, Wyles.

Doctor Lisa Tyne – Highly energetic compatriot to FJ and to a lesser extent Eston. Excitable but consciously exaggerates her natural proclivity towards ditziness. Top of her year at the Actavian academy in most sciences.

Duster – Real name Roland Sleeth. Young guardsman assigned to Vil following his investiture as Governor. Named after his valiant attempt at growing a moustache.

Elara Blanc – Close friends with both Toradan boys, but especially Cassus. Hopes for romantic entanglement. Natural leader, no nonsense, forthright, practical but feminine. Holds dual rank of Commander and Section Head. Not overly fond of droids. Gin fanatic.

Ensign Kel Fox – Fresh out of the Academy. Short and blond. Determined to succeed with the makings of a first rate pilot. Notched up more practice hours before launch than anyone else.

FJ (Frederick Jasper) – Chief scientist at Star City for twenty years. Knew the Toradon parents and still has a residual guilt for their disappearance. Possessor of a mighty and curious mind. Holds multiple degrees but regards the social sciences with something approaching contempt. Oldest member of the crew. Modest common sense. Fond of his stomach.

Flight Lieutenant Bob Scholes – Hailing from City-gens, Acto's most northerly settlement. Experienced pilot and a steady pair of hands. Frequently found in 3Bar with a beer or two.

Greggory Milson – One of the ten Regulators of the Central Computer Department (CCD) on Acto. Head of Atmospheric Control. Part of the 'Toradon gang' and loyal friend to Vil and Cassus. Provides valuable support to Vil following his temporary elevation to Governor.

Lucinda Grey – Section head for the hydroponic domes in City Gens, Acto's second city. Former conscript with Vil. Friends with Alan Spartan.

Mandy – A very rare, cutting edge RDX series droid from the tech world of Trestel. Inordinately expensive with capabilities banned on Earth and much of the Federation, she nevertheless demonstrates her worth and becomes an essential part of the crew.

Professor Eston Cousteau – Like Bronzemerit, originally from Earth. Travelled extensively as a younger man, visiting most of the major colonized systems, something that has grown rarer in more recent years. Eventually settled as a tenured professor at the Actavian Academy. Specialisms in Planetary Archaeology, botany & Zoology.

Senator Gilberto Temorri – One of the old guard of Senators. Amiable, benevolent and bald. A venerable man grown soft in his advancing years. Nominated by his fellow Senators as their representative aboard the Perga.

Senator Sejanus Lyron – Old enough to have personally known Cassus's predecessor, Governor Sendrick. Lyron revels in the privileges afforded to him as a Senator of the Actavian senate but with convictions as fickle as the wind. Nevertheless, a consummate politician and compelling orator with considerable sway in the Senate.

Sergeant Narcissa – Brox's NCO. Known as 'Narse'. Six foot tall and athletic. Catlike but surprisingly gentle and laid back until roused to savagery. Soft spot for elderly professors. And Brox.

Stuart Bronzemerit – Acto's favourite journalist. Originally hailing from Earth, Bronzemerit returned to Acto a year prior to the launch of the Perga to cover the story from within. Officially the *Head of News* aboard the Perga. Staunch Cassus supporter. Fond of snacks.

Vil Toradon – Cassus's brother. Former section head of tax Inspectorate of Acto city. Head of Star City operations and preparation of the frontier exploration ship, 'The Perga'. Interim Governor in Cassus's absence. Not as single minded as Cassus. Occasionally struggles with authority. Married to Lilia Toradan (ne Zara).

Wyles – Skilled mechanic and less talented sou chef. Runs the *Pergan Star* pub. Enamoured with the buxom form and culinary marvel that is Triple C.

List of Central Computer Department (CCD) Regulators

Acto's Regulators are the highest rung of the Central Computer Department (CCD) of the Core representing the five settlements of Acto.

1. Tax - Regulator Kathryn Gad
2. Hydroponics - Regulator Alan Spartan. Former section head of Acto's hydroponics domes.
3. Co-ordinator of the Secret Staff - Regulator Perterson
4. Atmospheric Control - Regulator Greggory Milson
5. Head of Acto's Planet Planning and Development (APPD) - Regulator Octavia Brinsmead
6. Transportation (PTTC) – Regulator Bill Dejean
7. Work & Welfare – Regulator Marta Mistral
8. Space Infrastructure – Regulator Conny Mann
9. Planetary Sanitation – Regulator Byrn
10. Planetary Education – Regulator Lilia Toradon (formerly Lilia Zara) – Vil's wife.

Influential Actavian Senators

Sejanus Lyron	Leader of the Lyron Faction
Allen Small	Lyron supporter
Gilberto Temorri	Representative of the Senate aboard the Perga
Aide to Senator Temorri	Dawn Haran
Guy Royal	Staunch Toradon supporter
Rosalind Corn	Toradon supporter
Alden Newberry	Neutral

Selected Section Heads (& Equivalent)

City Hydroponics	Lucinda Grey
Public Transport & Traffic Control (PTTC)	Teddy Ring
Commander of Acto's Security Force	Colonel Hill
Commander of the Toradon Navy	Captain Picton
Adjutant to the Head of Operations at Star City / Flight Safety Officer	Commander Elara Blanc
Star City Chief Coordinator	Vil Toradon

The Perga

Perga was an ancient Greek city in Anatolia, now Southwest Turkey, as well as the birthplace of Apollonius of Perga; a Greek astronomer and mathematician who wrote several books on Geometry. A handful of these works have survived to the modern day. Apollonius introduced several terms for conic sections that have been used in this book, including the name bestowed on the Toradon's parents' exploration ship - The *Ellipse*. The other two types of conic section are the hyperbola and the parabola.

From prow to stern the Perga is over a kilometre in length. The sleek shaft of its hull features two rotating rings; one at either end of the vessel. The first sits behind the bridge of the ship, the second two-thirds down the length of the ship in front of a huge deployable solar sail. The stern of the ship is dedicated to a bank of four powerful heat-exchange *Panther* class engines that sit in a square, two by two.

Unique in her development the Perga is the first of a new generation of deep space exploration ships. The bones of her sister ship are already being laid by the time Cassus and crew blast off into the unknown. The Perga is primarily an exploration ship but is highly customizable depending on the purpose of the mission. She can carry a crew of over one hundred people with further accommodation for two score of passengers and guests on a dedicated upper deck.

Although the Perga is not the largest space-faring ship ever devised or built by man she is amongst the most advanced, with development coming at huge cost over a very short period. The Perga is heavily armed with shipboard systems including four rotating Quadruple laser banks and several warheads including the latest *Spectral* class missiles. She is sufficiently massive to include a complement of four *Cohort* class fighters – The latest design out of a joint defense programme between Acto and the tech world of Trestel. The Cohorts are equipped with the small but potent *Lynx* class engine, a triple laser array and cluster missile pods or interchangeable guided missile systems. They are also capable of being deployed at a planetary level in atmospheric conditions.

For ground operations the Perga carries a number of squat cargo/landing ships known as 'Pugs' and several six-wheeled surface rovers as well as arrays of probes and deployable subspace transmitters. At the Governor's request the Perga also carries a contingent of sixty utility droids (RDG droids) and one incredibly advanced RDX series droid – The first of three such droids in the galaxy.

Ranks of the Actavian Defence Force
(Effectively the Infantry)

Second Lieutenant
Lieutenant
Captain
Major
Lieutenant Colonel
Colonel
General

Ranks of the Toradon Navy
(What we would refer to as the Airforce)

Acting / Ensign
Flight Lieutenant
Lieutenant Commander
Commander
Captain
Rear Admiral
Admiral

Printed in Great Britain
by Amazon